MW00990301

The Adventures of
Hamish and Mirren

The Adventures of
Hamish and Mirren

Magical Scottish Stories for Children

MOIRA MILLER

ILLUSTRATED BY
MAIRI HEDDERWICK

Kelpies is an imprint of Floris Books
This edition published by Floris Books, Edinburgh in 2015
First published in two volumes as *Hamish and the Wee Witch*
and *Hamish and the Fairy Gifts*
Third printing 2021
Text © 1986, 1988 Moira Miller
Illustrations © 1986, 1988 Mairi Hedderwick
Moira Miller and Mairi Hedderwick have asserted their
right under the Copyright, Designs & Patent Act 1988 to be
recognised as the Author and Illustrator of this Work
All rights reserved. No part of this book may be reproduced
without the prior permission of Floris Books, Edinburgh
www.florisbooks.co.uk

 Also available as an eBook

British Library CIP data available
ISBN 978-178250-211-1
Printed in Poland through Hussar

 Floris Books supports sustainable forest management by
printing this book on materials made from wood that
comes from responsible sources and reclaimed material

Contents

Hamish

Mither

Mirren

Introduction

The village of Camusbuie lies at the head of a silver sea loch on the west coast of Scotland.

There are three roads leading out of Camusbuie. The broad straight road marches to the south. The rough stony road struggles up the hillside to the Ben of Balvie, and the mountains beyond. But the third road meanders happily through the trees, down along the lochside where the sun dances on the water, and across a little wooden bridge over the Balvie Burn to a white farmhouse.

Before Mirren joins them, the farm is

home to Hamish and his old mother. She's always right, the old lady. Somehow she seems to know more than most people have ever forgotten. She even knows a good deal more than is usual about the Wee Folk and all the mischief they can brew up. Hamish used to smile at some of her stories, calling them fairy nonsense, but there came a time when he was very grateful indeed for what she knew.

Hamish and the Wee Witch

1.
Hamish and the Big Wind

It was a beautiful late summer evening. The sun had shone all day, warm and golden on the hayfield, dazzling on the little white cottage and dancing, sparkling and silver on the sea loch.

It was setting now in a glowing scarlet ball, filling the cottage kitchen with rosy light.

Hamish stretched his long legs out across the hearthrug, yawned and wiggled his toes in his socks.

"You great big clumsy tumshie!" grumbled his old mother, tripping over his feet. "Mind what you're doing." She leaned across him to stir the soup in the iron pot over the fire.

Hamish chuckled. He was happy after a good day's work, and even his old mother's scolding was not going to change that. From the crisp early morning mist to the long golden evening he had worked in the two green fields that ran from the farmhouse down to the shore of the loch. The rich grass he had cut and spread to dry in the sun was now piled up into two neat round haystacks by the byre. The animals would feed well through the long, cold winter months. Everything on the farm was quiet and peaceful. Just as it should be.

So Hamish stretched out his legs, rumpled his fair hair until it stood up like a corn stook above his rosy face, and smiled contentedly.

But not for long.

WHOOSH!

Suddenly with a crash and a cloud of black

smoke a great wind blew down the chimney into the room. The cat shot off the rug and ran squawking under the table. Hamish's old mother coughed and screeched and threw her apron over her face. The wind howled round the kitchen toppling cups and plates on the dresser, slammed the door open and stormed, roaring with laughter, out into the yard.

"Come back here, you great hooligan!" roared Hamish, struggling to pull on his boots. He tumbled out after the wind, and what a sight met his eyes.

The wooden bucket clattered noisily round and round on the cobble-stoned yard. The hen house, blown over on its side, was a screeching mass of feathers. The door of the byre crashed to and fro madly on its old hinges. Worst of all – the two neat round haystacks had gone.

Blown clear away with the Big Wind.

"What a mixter-maxter!" gasped Hamish, grabbing the bucket as it trundled past. He set to work to clear up, and all the time he raged about his haystacks.

"I'll get them back though," he growled. "Never you fear."

His old mother sniffed and shook her head.

"Your haystacks will be over the hills and far away by now," she said. "You'll never catch the Big Wind."

"Will I not?" said Hamish. "We'll soon see about that."

He pulled on his jerkin, took the stout leather bag that hung behind the door and filled it with bread, meat and cheese. He tied it firmly round the top with a length of rope and kissed his mother goodbye.

"What about your soup?" she shouted after him.

"Keep it till I get back," called Hamish, "*with* the haystacks."

She shook her head as she watched him march off through the heather up across the hill, following the path the wind had blown.

For miles and miles he walked, over high windswept moorland. He had finished most of the bread and had no meat or cheese left when he came upon a lonely farm cottage.

"Have you seen a Big Wind pass this way?" Hamish asked of the farmer.

The man stopped digging and leaned on his spade.

"Would that be the wind," said he, "that came by here the other night and made away with the thatched roof of my cowshed?"

"The very one," said Hamish. "He's away

with my two round haystacks and I'm after fetching them back. It may be that I can help you too."

"Then good luck to you, laddie," said the farmer. "For it's the long cold road you have to follow. You'll stop and have a bite to eat with us first."

Hamish set off again with his bag once more full of food. He walked on and on across hillside and glen, by river and loch until he came to a mill.

"Have you seen a Big Wind pass this way?" Hamish asked of the miller.

The man put down the heavy bag of grain he was carrying and stood up, stretching his back.

"Would that be the wind," said he, "that came by here the other night and made away with my wheelbarrow?"

"The very one," said Hamish. "He's away with my two round haystacks and I'm after fetching them back. It may be that I can help you too."

"Then good luck to you, laddie," said the miller. "For it's the long cold road you have to follow. You'll stop and have a bite to eat with me first."

Having eaten and rested Hamish set off once more and came at last to a little dairy by the roadside. In the cool white kitchen a young girl was stirring cream in a big wooden churn to make butter.

"Have you seen a Big Wind pass this way?" Hamish asked of the dairymaid.

"Would that be the wind," said she, "that whistled through my garden the other night and made away with my best petticoat from the washing line?"

"The very one," said Hamish. "He's taken my two round haystacks and I'm after fetching them back. It may be that I can help you too."

The dairymaid looked him up and down, and giggled. "Then you're the very lad they're looking for up at the castle," said she. "The Laird himself has offered a rich reward to the man who can catch the Big Wind."

"Indeed?" said Hamish.

"Half his gold and silver," said the dairymaid.

"Fancy that!" said Hamish.

"And one of his daughters to marry," sniffed the dairymaid. "Hoity toity misses!"

Hamish laughed, gave her a kiss on the cheek and asked the way to the castle.

In the great hall the Laird sat at dinner with his three daughters. The two older ones ignored Hamish completely, but the youngest one, with long golden pigtails and freckles like new pennies, offered him a stool and a cup of wine.

"That's the way, Mirren," said the Laird. "Come away in, laddie. Sit down and tell us your story." He listened carefully while Hamish told the story of his haystacks, and how he was determined to win them back again, along with the reward.

"Aye, well," said the Laird, "there's some fine young men have come after the reward. And gone home again in a very sorry state... very sorry indeed..." He shook his head and stared gloomily at his daughters.

"Och, Father," said the oldest one, "they were none of them grand enough to marry *us* anyway."

"One day," said the second daughter, looking down her nose at Hamish, "a *real* prince will come and claim the reward – and *my* hand in marriage." She stared dreamily into her pudding.

"He will not!" screamed the first daughter,

thumping the table till the plates jumped. "He'll want *me*."

The Laird sighed, shook his head and led Hamish over to the window.

The old grey stone castle stood on a cliff top overlooking the sea, which lapped grey and cold on the rocks beneath them.

"Do you see yon island out there?" said the Laird.

Through the evening mirk Hamish could just make out the jagged shape of a small island in the bay. Looming above the rocks, and seeming almost to have grown from them, there stood an old ruined tower.

"I see it," said Hamish.

"That's where the Big Wind is to be found," said the Laird. "When he's not out and about stirring up a shindig like that pair there!" At the table his two older daughters were still squabbling.

Hamish laughed and winked at Mirren.

"Leave this to me," said he. "I'll soon see him off!"

The Laird offered Hamish a suit of armour for protection, but it was so long since it had been used that the hinges were rusted solid. Mirren found him an old helmet, but Hamish only roared with laughter.

"It's big enough to make soup for the village in!"

Taking only a small boat and his big leather bag he rowed himself out to the island, and slept that night on the beach.

He awoke with the first light of day, stretched and sat up – and what a surprise met him then. In the still morning the island held its breath. There was no sign of the Big Wind, but tumbled all about him lay gates and fences, shed roofs and wheelbarrows.

Amongst them with the dairymaid's petticoat draped on top, were his two neat round haystacks.

Hamish was struggling to load them into the boat when the sky suddenly darkened.

There came a distant whistling and roaring like a huge dragon. The sea around the island tossed and boiled, the waves twisted and crashed on the pebble beach. In a great swirling of spray the Big Wind shrieked across the island.

"Oooooooo - HOooooooo!"

he roared. "And where do you think you're going with these, young sir?"

"Taking them home, where they belong," said Hamish calmly, carrying on as if nothing had happened.

"O-oh-ho, you're not!" roared the Big Wind.

"O-oh-ho, yes I *am!*" said Hamish.

"And you can puff till you're blue in the face, but you'll not stop me."

The Big Wind, whipped to a frenzy, whirled himself into a huge black cloud and raged down. Hamish dropped the hay and jumped neatly aside. The Wind crashed into the wall behind him.

"Can't catch me for a wee bawbee!" sang Hamish rudely.

The Big Wind gathered himself into a screaming rage. Then there followed such a racing and chasing all around the island and the ruined tower. Hamish jumped in and out of doorways, up and down stairways, in and out through empty windows, with the Big Wind in pursuit. But wherever the Big Wind pounced, Hamish had been – and gone.

"Stand still you cheeky wee limmer!" roared the Wind, whirling into a hurricane.

"Now I'm here, now I'm there, but you

cannae catch me anywhere," sang Hamish.

He dodged, laughing and panting, into the hall of the old tower. In front of him the huge fireplace stood, black and empty, and at his heels the Big Wind screamed in fury. Hamish looked quickly round the room.

There was nowhere to turn.

"Aaaaaaaa-haaaaa, I've got you now!" shrieked the Big Wind. "Just wait till I catch hold of you!"

Hamish ran for the fireplace, dodging and weaving, and scrambled up the great empty chimney. Higher and higher, faster and faster he climbed until at last he struggled out at the top, gasping for breath. Behind him the Big Wind snatched at his heels.

Quick as a flash Hamish grabbed his leather bag, opened it wide, and held it over the chimney top.

"Oooooooo - HOOOOOOOO!"

roared the Big Wind in terrifying triumph – and whistled straight into Hamish's big leather bag. It was a second's work for him to tie the rope with three tight knots and stuff the bag back into the chimney. As he climbed back down the outside of the old tower he could hear the wind howling and struggling to be set free.

When the story of how Hamish had tricked the Big Wind became known, people came from far and wide to claim their stolen belongings. Some of them just came to look at the tower and listen to the Wind howling in the chimney. They were shown round the island by the Laird's two older daughters, who had moved across to live there.

"Because after all," said the oldest, "one of these days a *real* prince might come sight-seeing. Who knows? And when he does come he'll fall in love with me – on the instant…"

"*Rubbish!*" screamed the younger one, stamping her foot. "How could he possibly – you ugly old bat!"

All day long their voices echoed round the island and faintly back across the sea to where the Laird sat smiling peacefully in his castle.

Mirren smiled too. She smiled and tossed her long pigtails and said "yes" when Hamish asked to marry her. The party lasted for a month and a day, with feasting and dancing in the castle and the village. Even the dairymaid, who was invited, had to admit that Hamish had chosen a beautiful bride – who was not in the least bit stuck up.

After a time, however, Hamish began to miss his home, so one fine morning he and Mirren said goodbye to the Laird, who would have been very unhappy had it not been for the fact that the dairymaid had agreed to stay on at the castle as his housekeeper.

Hamish and Mirren packed all their belongings, loaded the neat round haystacks into a cart, and set off back to the wee farmhouse and the two green fields that ran down to the shining silver sea loch.

2.
Hamish and the Wee Witch

Hamish and Mirren came home to the farm, all set to live happily ever after.

But sometimes things don't work out like that.

Mirren loved the little white house on the hillside. Every morning she ran out into the fields where the fresh taste of the sea mingled with the warm smell of the wild flowers. She laughed to see how the fat brown hens came running to greet her.

"Here, here. Chook chook chook," she called, scattering corn like golden rain from the big basket. The hens fussed around her feet, pecking and squabbling as she called to them. The eggs they laid for Mirren seemed bigger and browner and the yolks more golden than ever before.

"Mmmmm, she's no' bad – for a laird's daughter," sniffed Hamish's old mother. "But do you think she can milk a cow?"

Hamish laughed as he watched Mirren dance round the farmyard among the hens.

"Of course she can!" he said. "My wee Mirren can do anything."

And he was just about right. Very soon Mirren was milking the cow as well and the big wooden bucket was filled to the top every day with rich creamy milk.

"You're a treasure," said Hamish, "and I wouldna' change you for all the gold and silver in your father's kists."

Mirren laughed and went on about her work, singing like the thrush in the hawthorn bush. Even Hamish's old mother had to admit that the farm was a brighter and happier place.

It seemed as if it would always be like that, and they would live happily ever after. but suddenly one day, there came a change.

Mirren stopped singing.

She came in from the byre after the morning milking with the big wooden pail only half full.

"Och, Mirren," said Hamish. "Is the wee cow not well?"

"I don't know," said Mirren, puzzled and upset. "She seems restless and unhappy, and though I begged for more, that was all the milk she had to give."

"Well never mind, Mirren," said Hamish. "Maybe she'll do better in the morn, and if anyone can help her, you can."

But the next morning it was the same story. The wee cow only gave half a bucket of milk, and that so thin and weak it might as well have been water from the loch.

Mirren was very unhappy.

"No sense in crying over the milk," said Hamish trying to comfort her. "I'll see what I can do." That evening he took the bucket and went out to the byre.

As he stepped from the back door into the yard he was just in time to hear a scuffling sound, and catch a glimpse of a little old woman in a green cloak. In her hurry to leave she caught the cloak on a nail by the byre door.

"WHIGMALEERIES!"

she hooted, and pulled at the cloth to free herself. As she did so Hamish could see that she was carrying a wooden pail. And that pail was full to the brim with rich creamy milk.

"Here!" called Hamish running after her.
"That's my milk you're after stealing."

The little old woman whirled round and
fixed him with a bright beady green eye.

"Away ye go," she croaked, pointing a
finger like a twisted twig, "or I'll turn you
into a toad!"

Hamish stepped back into the cottage
and slammed the door shut as she vanished
in a cloud of evil-smelling black smoke.

"We have to stop her," he said to his mother
and Mirren as they sat down to supper later
that evening. "But how?"

Mirren shook her head. She was at a loss
to know what to do. Hamish turned to his
mother. She was older and wiser and knew
about these things.

"That woman is one of the Wee Folk," she
said. "And it'll no' be easy to stop her, I'm
thinking. But there is a way." She got up and
looked quickly round the cottage – under

the table and up the chimney – then closing the door tight shut she came back and sat down.

"I've never tried it myself," she whispered, "but they do say that if you can find out the name of a wee witch then she'll have no power to cast a spell over you."

"Then we must find her name," said Mirren, "and send her back where she came from."

But that was not so easy. For days she and Hamish went round their neighbours asking if anyone knew of the old woman. They found that although she had stolen eggs from this one, and butter from that, nobody could help. They, none of them, knew who she was.

"We'll go down to Camusbuie," said Hamish. "There may be someone in the village who can help." But even old Biddy who kept the shop, and knew all the gossip before it happened, was no help at all.

And every day the wee old witch came back to fill her bucket with stolen milk.

At last Hamish's old mother had had enough. She liked nothing better than rich creamy milk with a plate of porridge and she was missing it very much.

She put down her spoon with a bang on the breakfast table. Hamish and Mirren jumped.

"I'll soon sort this out," she said. Pulling her shawl tightly round her she stamped out to the byre.

"Here, Mother!" shouted Hamish, running after her. "She'll do something terrible!"

"Just let her try!" sniffed Hamish's mother. She slammed open the byre door and there, sure enough, sat the wee old witch. She was perched on the old milking stool, rocking gently from side to side and crooning a strange song as she milked the wee cow into her big bucket.

"Out of there, you!" screamed Hamish's mother. "You can't even milk a cow properly. Look at the way you're doing it – all back side hindmost. No wonder the poor beast's upset!" She barged in, knocking the old witch off her milking stool.

Hamish jumped back out of the way as she rolled over at his feet in a dirty green bundle.

"How dare you!" howled the old witch, her feet waving in the air. "I've been milking cows for three hundred and forty-nine years. Are you trying to tell me I don't know what I'm doing?"

"Just that," said Hamish's mother firmly. "Now get out of the way and let me get on with it."

The wee old witch staggered to her feet, her face purple with rage, her straggly hair stuck full of straw.

"I'll turn you into a toad!" she screamed, struggling to get up again.

"Aye, well if you're as good at that as you are at milking, I'll not be too bothered," said Hamish's mother, calmly sitting down on the milking stool.

"WHIGMALEERIES!"

shrieked the furious wee witch, gasping for breath. "I'll make you sorry about this. I will that! You'll live to regret this or… or my name's not – *Grizelda Grimithistle!*"

There was silence.

Hamish stared at his mother, who smiled and nodded.

"Grizelda Grimithistle is it? Well, well, fancy that," she said smugly.

Hamish roared with laughter at the sight of the wee witch's face.

"Much obliged to you for telling us, Grizelda Grimithistle," he said. "And now that we know, you'll not be stealing any more milk."

"You can forget the eggs and butter from down the road too," said his mother.

The wee old witch was livid with fury. She screamed and stamped and spun round in such a temper that she rolled herself into a huge green ball. Still screeching and howling she whirled out of the byre and up over the hill, burning a path through the heather that is still there to this day.

Down in Camusbuie they said afterwards that her howls could be heard clear across the Seven Glens and the echoes rolled like thunder round the top of the Ben of Balvie all that day.

"I don't doubt we've seen the last of Grizelda Grimithistle on this farm," said

Hamish's old mother as she picked up the bucket of rich creamy milk for her porridge. And so she was right – well almost.

3.
Hamish and the Pedlar's Pipe

Hamish and Mirren had been down in the village of Camusbuie for the day. Hamish had sold all his cheese and butter, and bought a fine new iron pot to hang on the hook over the fire. Mirren had sold her eggs and the soft woollen shawls that Hamish's old mother had knitted during the long winter months. She had bought herself a red woollen skirt and they were singing as they marched back up the road home.

The path they took wound up from the village, round the heather-covered shoulder of the Ben of Balvie. The Ben was so high that there were days, even in summer, when the top was hidden in thick white clouds. But now the sun was shining and the Ben stood crisp against the pure blue of a cloudless sky.

Mirren ran through the long grass by the path, picking wild flowers. Meadowsweet and buttercup she gathered by the armful.

Suddenly she stopped and stood quite still.

"What is it?" called Hamish from the path behind her.

"Shhhh," said Mirren. "Can you not hear it?"

They stood together on the quiet sunlit path. At first Hamish heard nothing, but then Mirren smiled.

"Listen," she whispered. From far off, away beyond the happy chirping of the birds, came a strange little tune, silvery and clear.

The music was slow and gentle, and although it was far off, at the same time it seemed to be all around them. It whispered, dancing like the butterflies through the trees and the thick green grass. It was hard to tell whether the tune was sad or happy – or both. Mirren stood spellbound.

"My, it's that bonny," she whispered.

"It's the Wee Folk," said Hamish and he held tight to his new iron pot. Everyone knows that if you have something of iron about you then the Wee Folk are unable to weave their spells.

"No," laughed Mirren. "It's just a travelling pedlar. Look!"

Sure enough, round the corner of the path, down from the Ben came a strange figure.

He seemed tall at first, but then Hamish noticed he was not much bigger than Mirren. He wore a long brown swirling cloak that seemed almost to float behind him. A huge shady brown hat with a curling feather hid most of his face.

Under the brim of the hat they could see that his hair was thick and dark, and that his bright brown eyes seemed to dance and twinkle in time with his music.

The stranger was playing the haunting music on a thin silver pipe.

"Fine evening," called Hamish. "You fair startled us. That's a rare tune you're playing."

"Ah, it's the fine flute, sir, that does it," said the pedlar. He stopped on the path in front of them and smiled with his head tilted to one side. "I could sell you this for just one of those six gold coins you earned today."

"How did you know about the gold?" said Hamish, but the pedlar ignored him and turned, smiling, to Mirren.

"It will make music to have your old slippers dancing on the hearthrug," he said. "And the birds themselves will stop singing to listen." He put the flute to his lips again and trilled a tune like a blackbird's. Fine clear notes that tumbled over each other in sheer happiness.

"My, but that is bonny," whispered Mirren.

"Here," said the pedlar. "Take it, and welcome."

Before Hamish knew what had happened he was standing with the pipe in his hand and the pedlar was off down the path with one of his gold coins.

"Just a minute," Hamish shouted after him. "I can't play this. Tell me – how do I make music with it?"

The pedlar turned back, laughing.

"That's a gift that's given to the man with a kind heart," he called, "and the breath to blow clear through the Ben of Balvie."

"Blow through the Ben?" shouted Hamish, angry now. "Yon's not possible! Here you – give me my money back…"

But the pedlar had vanished, and although Hamish and Mirren searched high and low through the trees and along the path, all they saw was the dancing lace of the shadows. All they heard was the sweet song of the birds.

"Never mind, Hamish," said Mirren at last. "Maybe you can learn how to play the wee pipe yourself."

"Aye, maybe," sighed Hamish. He put the pipe to his lips and blew, but the only sound that came out was a high piercing whistle that hurt the ears.

Night after night Hamish sat by the fire blowing at his pipe. Mirren tried as well. But there was no way they could make music as the pedlar had.

"Mercy on us," screeched his old mother. "That's more like a parcel of cats fighting in the barn! Put the thing away laddie, afore we're all deaf."

Sadly, Hamish put the little pipe in his

pouch and forgot all about it – until some weeks later.

It happened that he was up on the slopes of the Ben of Balvie, bringing down his sheep, when he remembered the pipe again.

"It can hardly bother anyone if I play it up here," he said to himself. The shining silver of the little pipe was dull, from having lain forgotten in his pouch. Hamish breathed on it, and rubbed it on his shirtsleeve.

He took a deep breath, put the pipe to his lips, and blew. But though he blew until his face was red as the sunset and there was no puff left in him, the little silver pipe only squeaked and howled as before.

"Good gracious, laddie, what a caterwauling," came a voice behind him.

Hamish spun round, and came face to

face with a wee old woman. Smaller than his own mother, but plumper, she stood in the heather with a large round bundle wrapped in an old green shawl at her feet.

"Where did you come from?" said Hamish. "I don't mind seeing you on the path."

"Aye, well seen that," said the old woman. Then she smiled at him. "You look like a big strong lad. Before you blow yourself clean to bits, I'd be much obliged if you could give me a wee bit of help. I've been on a visit to my grandson and now I find I'm locked out of my house."

"No trouble," said Hamish. "You lead me there, and I'll soon get you in."

"It's this way," said the wee old woman. "Follow me." She picked up her skirts and set off climbing towards the top of the Ben.

"And bring my bundle with you!" she called back.

"Aye, right," laughed Hamish, swinging it

up onto his shoulder. His knees buckled as he almost sank under the weight.

"How did you ever manage to lift this?" he gasped, amazed. But the wee old woman was away, striding ahead of him. Hamish hoisted the bundle onto his broad shoulder and set off after her.

Higher and higher they climbed up the rocky slope. There was no sign of house or cottage but the wee old woman marched on so Hamish had to follow. Up among the mist and clouds they climbed. With the damp striking cold through his shirt and the bundle becoming heavier and heavier, Hamish staggered to a halt, panting.

"Guidsakes, laddie," fussed the old woman, coming back down through the mist. "Pick up your feet will you. We'll never get there this night!"

Wearily Hamish dragged the bundle up again and stumbled on. At last, just as the last of his strength had gone and he knew he could climb no further, the old woman stopped and turned to him.

"Right, laddie, we're here now," she said. "Set it down, careful mind! There's things in that shawl that all the riches in the world could never buy."

Hamish gently lowered the bundle and stared around. In front of him the bleak rocky mountainside vanished into the mist. To the right a great slope of small stones and gravel swept down like a waterfall of rock, and to his left rose a sheer cliff face.

"Are you sure this is where you live?" he gasped, amazed.

"Do you think I don't know my own front door?" sniffed the old woman indignantly. "Now you take out that pipe, laddie, and blow. Blow as long and as loud as ever you can."

Hamish took out his silver pipe, drew in a deep breath, and blew.

He blew a fine high piercing note that could have been heard clear over the Ben and down to Camusbuie. The note echoed up the hillside and rang back off the rocks, louder and louder, as if it would never stop.

And in the high clear ringing tone of the flute, the rocks in front of Hamish seemed to melt away. The grey towering cliff face dissolved into a deep cave lit by a soft green shimmering light.

Hamish stopped blowing, and stood open-mouthed as the echoes died around him.

The wee old woman nodded, picked up her bundle as if it had been light as a feather, and stepped into the cave. Around her, shadowy silvery figures came and went, flitting soundlessly.

The woman who turned back to Hamish was no longer old. She was young, and beautiful, and smiling.

"Aye, we did right to give you that pipe," she chuckled. "You've a kind heart and the breath to blow clear through the Ben. Now away home with you and blow your pipe. Blow it for all the world to hear."

The green light of the cave faded. Hamish blinked, and found himself staring at the grey rocks. A wisp of cloud trailed across the cliff face, and the sun broke through, warming his back.

He turned then and ran, leaping from stone to stone, slipping and sliding, panting for breath. Away from the cloud-wrapped top of the Ben he ran, back down the mountainside.

At last he tumbled onto the grassy slope above the path that led to home, and lay panting. The sun, breaking through the patch in the clouds, suddenly shone down on Camusbuie, the loch and his tiny white house far below.

Hamish picked himself up, brushing the grass from his clothes.

"I doubt I must have been dreaming," he said, shaking his head. It would have taken hours to climb the Ben, and above his head the sun was still high in the sky.

He laughed and set off to walk down the grassy slope. As he went he took the silver pipe from his pouch, put it to his lips and blew.

By the time he reached the cottage his fingers were skipping on the little flute to a tune that would have made your old slippers dance on the hearthrug.

Even the very birds in the trees had stopped singing to listen in wonder.

4.
Mirren and the Spring Cleaning

It all started because Mirren was in a bit of a bad mood.

She had been working on the farm, and in the byre, and what with one thing and another had not been able to make a start on the spring cleaning in the cottage.

One night, when Hamish's old mother had gone off to bed early, he and Mirren were peacefully toasting their toes in front of the fire. Hamish yawned and stretched. Mirren, who had been fidgeting in her chair all evening, suddenly jumped up.

"If I don't start now," she said, "it'll never

get done!" She grabbed the broom and swept the rug so hard that great clouds of dust flew up around her.

Hamish sneezed and the cat shot off under the corner cupboard.

"Here Mirren," panted Hamish, between sneezes. "It's far too late for that. Nobody does a spring cleaning at bedtime."

"Stuff!" said Mirren, lifting the rug and shaking it.

AAAAAAAA-CHOOO!

Hamish gave a sneeze that rattled the china dogs on the mantelpiece.

"You can sit there till the cows come home if you like," said Mirren. "But this spring cleaning is going to get done."

Hamish sat on by the fire for a time as she polished and dusted around him. He shifted his chair three times so that Mirren could sweep underneath it. When she rolled up her sleeves and filled a bucket of water Hamish decided that he had had enough.

"I think I'll leave you to get on with it," he said, tiptoeing through the puddles. "I'm away to bed."

But Mirren heard never a word. She was scrubbing and polishing as though her life depended on it.

She took down all the curtains and left them to soak in a tub of clean water. She shook up the old patchwork cushions until the feathers flew like a snowstorm. She scrubbed and rubbed at the best copper kettle until her own face was smiling back, round and golden brown, with the one wee dimple where the kettle had a dent in it.

It was while she was polishing the face of the old wag-at-the-wa clock that Mirren suddenly realised that the time was almost midnight.

In the big bedroom Hamish was snoring softly, while in the wee room at the back his old mother muttered something to herself in her sleep, turned over and settled down again.

Mirren looked around her. There still seemed so much to be done. In the quietness of the night the big clock chimed twelve. Mirren dried her hands, stretched her back, and sighed.

"Oh that someone would come,
From land or sea,
From far or near
With help for me."

Now at midnight that is a dangerous thing to do, for the Wee Folk are always around somewhere – and always listening. And that was just the sort of invitation they could never resist.

No sooner had Mirren said the words, and the twelfth chime still echoing round the little room, than there was a knock on the door.

"Mercy on us!" Mirren jumped. "Who can that be at this time of the night?"

"Open the door to me, Mirren my lass," came a strange voice. "You begged for help and the time that I have will be yours alone."

Mirren opened the door, just a crack, and came face to face with a fat little man.

His untidy white beard half hid a face that was crinkled and brown like a walnut. He hitched up his baggy brown tunic, and before Mirren could say another word had shoved open the door and stepped into the cottage.

"Aye," he said, glancing round and pushing up his sleeves. "We'll soon have you set to rights, lass." He grabbed the bucket of water and set to, scrubbing the floor all over again.

"Here, stop, I've done that…" Mirren started to say when there came another knock at the door. In barged two old women wearing green aprons and big wooden clogs. They snatched the cushions from the chairs and plumped and pulled at them.

"Stop it!" yelled Mirren, trying to grab the cushions. But she might as well have been talking to the clock.

After that came another knock at the door, then another and another, until at last the whole house was full of Wee Folk all falling over each other, kicking over buckets of water, knocking over ornaments and generally creating a shambles in the tidy little kitchen.

Mirren stared in horror.

She raced into the bedroom and shook Hamish, but he was deep asleep. The harder she shook him, the louder he snored. It was as if he slept the sleep of the enchanted.

"Please," she begged the Wee Folk. "Please will you stop!"

"Aye, well," said one of the old ladies. "I

wouldn't mind a wee cup of tea about now."

Mirren quickly stirred up the fire and set the kettle to boil.

"I'll just have the buttermilk," said the little old man who had arrived first.

"Try some of the shortbread," screeched another voice. "It's not bad – considering."

Before Mirren could stop them, the Wee Folk had eaten and drunk everything they could lay their hands on. Even the porridge that Mirren had put to simmer for breakfast by the side of the fire had gone.

And no sooner was it finished than they went back to work with a will, scrubbing and polishing like mad things. One wee woman grabbed the big wooden bucket in which the curtains were soaking and started to scrub down the cupboard with them.

"No – no!" howled Mirren, trying to pull the bucket away, but the wee woman held on tightly.

"It's no trouble, lassie," she screeched. "I like to see a job well done." She dunked the curtains back in the dirty water, soaking herself and Mirren, and went on scrubbing.

Mirren was desperate. She had to stop them somehow before they ruined her little home – but how?

"Hamish's mother!" she whispered to herself. Like many old people Hamish's mother seemed to know more about the Wee Folk than most.

The old lady lay on her back, a big white frilly nightcap pulled down over her hair, and a soft knitted shawl about her shoulders. Mirren shook her gently.

"Eh – eh… two plain, two purl…" muttered the old lady. Mirren shook her a little harder. The old lady snuffled like a hedgehog and turned over on her side.

"Please, mother, wake up," hissed Mirren. "It's the Wee Folk. I can't get rid of them."

Hamish's mother sat up and pulled the shawl tight around her shoulders. She listened as Mirren told her what had happened.

"Aye, well, if you did your spring cleaning in the daytime like the rest of the world…" said the old lady. Mirren sniffed into her handkerchief.

"I can't get them out of the house," she wailed. "They won't go until they've finished."

"We'll soon see about that," said Hamish's mother. "You slip out the back door, and stand on that wee bit hillock over by the hawthorn tree. Then when I wave you'll shout – as loud as you can, mind now."

"But what do I shout?" asked Mirren.

"I'm coming to that," said the old lady crossly. "You'll shout, 'Dun Shee is on fire!' Shout three times, loud and clear. That'll soon get them out."

"But why? What's Dun Shee?" asked Mirren, perplexed.

"Bless me," said the old lady. "Don't you know anything? Dun Shee is the name they have for their own Fairy Hill where they live. If they think it's on fire they'll be out of this house quicker than you can wink!"

So Mirren did as she was told. She crept quietly out of the back door and climbed the wee hillock. Around her the night sky was dark and still – even the stars slept. Behind her, from inside the cottage, she could hear the crashing, banging and yells of the Wee Folk.

Mirren took a deep breath and shouted at the top of her voice, "Dun Shee is on fire! Dun Shee is on fire! Dun Shee is on fire!"

Out they rushed, falling over each other in their hurry. Screeching and squawking like hens with a fox after them, scattering brooms, buckets and dusters as they went.

They tumbled off up the hill in a great noisy green whirlwind.

Mirren waited until she was sure the last one had gone. She ran back into the cottage, bolted the door behind her and pushed the big kitchen table across the front to jam it shut.

"It worked!" she panted. "They've gone. We've done it."

"Aye, but they'll be back, mark my words," said Hamish's mother. "And they'll be ill-pleased when they find we've tricked them. But we'll be ready for them – we'll be ready."

No sooner had she said that than there came a sound like a great rushing of wind and a pounding on the door.

"Let us in, Mirren. Let us in!" called the voices. "We've not done yet, and you'll not keep us out."

"Go away!" shouted Mirren. "Oh please go away!"

But the voices went on calling, kicking and pounding on the door.

"Let us in!" echoed the voices down the chimney. Hamish's mother stirred the fire to a blaze and piled on more peat, stirring up the smoke. Outside there was coughing and sneezing – and then silence.

"What are they doing do you think?" whispered Mirren.

Suddenly the broom jumped up from the rug and swept round the room in a mad dance.

"So that's the way it's to be," said Hamish's mother. "Mirren, fetch some of those big iron nails that Hamish used to mend the fence. Hurry now."

Mirren found the bag of nails and the big hammer.

"Right now," said the old woman. "The Wee Folk can never cast a spell where there is cold iron. You put a nail in the handle of that broom."

But that was easier said than done. The broom jinked and jouked around the furniture, behind the cupboards, and even into the bedroom. Mirren chased after it, climbing over the bed, and still Hamish slept on, snoring gently. At last she trapped the broom in a corner of the kitchen.

"Quickly!" she shouted. "The hammer." She held on grimly as the broom danced madly round the room, dragging her with it. Hamish's mother grabbed the handle and in the end it took the two of them to get it down onto the floor. They sat one on each end while Mirren banged in a nail.

The broom lay still and quiet and as ordinary as it had ever been.

Mirren sat on the floor, puffing and panting. Before she had time to catch her breath, however, the dusters started up. They flew round the room, rubbing and polishing everything they touched – the table, the cupboard, the mantelpiece.

"Get off!" screeched the old lady as they flew at her like great coloured seagulls. Mirren leapt and jumped, trying to catch them. The clock was polished so hard it chimed thirteen times, and still they flew round and round the room.

"The kist!" shouted the old woman, catching one of the china dogs as it fell from the mantelpiece. "Get them into the kist! It's made of rowan wood, and the Wee Folk's magic can't abide that."

The dusters by this time were rolling about beneath the big cupboard, fighting like a pair of cats. Mirren poked at them with a knitting pin.

"I've got them," she yelled, grabbing a handful of cloth.

The old woman opened the lid of the big rowan-wood chest and Mirren stuffed two of the dusters in. The third duster, twisting out of her hand, flew crazily round the room above their heads.

Mirren swiped at it with the broom. The old woman stood on the stool and screeched at it to come down immediately. The duster flapped round cheekily, just out of reach.

At last Mirren managed to jump high enough to grab a corner. She pulled it over to the chest, opened the lid just a crack and, stuffing it in, flopped down breathless on top. In the quiet room the only sounds were the old clock and her gasping breath.

Outside, the night was over.

The early morning filled the sky with a clear pearly blue. The cockerel called from the yard and the cows mooed softly to each other in the byre.

Far off in the distance the gentle sea lapped on the beach, and down by the village a dog barked as the first threads of smoke snaked lazily up from cottage chimneys.

"Have they gone?" whispered Mirren hoarsely.

"Aye," said the old woman, "but they've had their fun."

Mirren and the old lady flopped down in the chairs by the fireside, exhausted, as the early morning sun creeping through the windows lit the tiny kitchen, and filled the bedroom with brightness.

Hamish woke at last, stretched and yawned.

"My, that was a rare sleep," he called through to Mirren as he dressed. "I don't know when…"

And then he stood – and stopped, and stared.

He stared at his mother and Mirren, sound asleep on either side of the cold fireplace.

He stared at the empty porridge pot tipped on the floor.

He stared in amazement at the sink full of dirty dishes and the little kitchen, usually so tidy, and now such a shambles.

"Mirren," he gasped. "What on earth have you been doing all night?"

Mirren stirred, then settled herself more comfortably in the big chair.

"Spring cleaning," she muttered – and went back to sleep again.

5.
Hamish and the Sea Urchin

The weather had been wild and stormy for days. The wind played a mad dance in the trees around Hamish's farmhouse and whistled down the chimney into the fireplace so that the flames flickered and jumped unevenly round the bottom of the iron kettle.

Every night, as they lay snug in bed, Hamish and Mirren listened to the sea roaring on the rocks.

"I don't like it," whispered Mirren in the dark.

"Och, it's just the spring tides," said Hamish. "It happens every year. The tide comes up further and further each day – but then it goes out further as well. One day it'll go out as far as it can and then after that it will come back to being the same as always. You'll see, Mirren, don't worry. Go to sleep."

Mirren lay and listened to the huge waves crashing on the rocks and tearing at the seaweed on the shore, and she pulled the big blanket up over her head and went back to sleep.

Early next morning she yawned and stretched.

After the days of stormy weather the sun was shining again, the wild screaming wind had gone. Everything was still. There was no sound – not even the waves crashing on the beach.

Mirren leapt out of bed and ran to the window.

"Hamish, come quick!" she called. "The sea's gone. It's not there any more. What's happened? Hamish, wake up, you dozy lump. What's happened?"

Hamish climbed out of bed sleepily and came to the window. Before the house, instead of the silver sheet of the loch stretching away between the hills to the distant shimmering blue line of the sea, there was only sand. Miles and miles of shining wet sand.

"My, the tide's fairly gone out this time," said Hamish, scratching his head. "There's rocks out there I've never seen before."

"Fancy that," whispered Mirren.

"Nobody's ever set foot out there," said Hamish. "I've a mind to do it myself before the tide comes back in, just to say I've walked down the loch."

"It isn't safe," grumbled his old mother over breakfast. Hamish laughed and took a stout walking stick from the basket by the door.

"Don't say I didn't warn you," she grumbled, stumping back to her chair by the fireside.

But Hamish was away, striding out across the wet sand, stopping now and then to look at the things the sea had left behind as it swept out of the loch. He picked up a pretty pebble and put it in his pouch for Mirren. Then on he went again, across the wet firm sand, leaving footprints where no footprints had ever been seen before.

Out towards the middle of the loch where the sand was softest lay a clump of black weed-covered rocks. Hamish clambered over the slippery surface, searching in pools and cracks for the tiny plants and sea creatures normally hidden in the depths of the cold blue loch.

"Ach, drat it!"

came a voice from behind a rock.

Hamish straightened up and looked around. There was not another soul to be seen, and no other footprint but his own on the smooth wet sand.

"Och, for goodness' sake!" came the voice again, squeaky and grumpy like a bad-tempered old man.

"Who's there?" called Hamish, searching around the rocks.

"Who do you think? You daft gomeril!"

Hamish walked right round the rocks. There was nobody in sight. He stopped and looked about him, thoroughly puzzled.

"Mind where you're putting your great big feet!"

Hamish looked down, and there behind the rocks lay a huge sea urchin. It was easily the biggest sea urchin that Hamish

had ever seen. His great rounded grey and pink shell was covered with crusty knobs and spikes.

"I beg your pardon," said Hamish. "I didn't see you lying about down there."

"Obviously not," grumbled the urchin. "That's the trouble with you folk that have feet. Think you can put them anywhere. Ech – humph!" The sea urchin tried to move himself along the rock, but only managed to roll over onto the sand.

"Are you – eh – in trouble?" asked Hamish politely.

"Well you don't think I'm sitting around here for fun, do you?" said the sea urchin rudely. "The tide's gone out and left me high and dry. High and dry! I'm trying to get back to the water."

Hamish stood up and, shading his eyes with his hand, peered down the loch to the faint blue line of the sea.

"You've a fair wee bit to go," he said. "Here, let me give you a hand."

"Aye, well, as long as they're not as clumsy as your feet," grunted the urchin ungraciously.

Hamish bent to pick him up. The sea urchin was quite taken by surprise, he had never been handled before, and shot out all his bristles.

"Yee-ouch!" yelled Hamish, dropping him and stepping back quickly.

"Clumsy big tumshie," snorted the sea urchin. "You're worse than a walrus."

"It's your own fault," said Hamish, feeling a bit peeved. "Can you not fold up your spikes or something?"

The sea urchin sniffed, but he folded his spikes back flat against the shell. Very carefully, Hamish picked him up in his two hands and set off across the sand. He picked his way slowly round the wet rocks, past the pools. As he went the sea urchin moaned and complained all the time.

"Och, be careful, will you," and, "Mind what you're doing, you great gormless lump!"

"I'm trying to help but you're not making it very easy," snapped Hamish.

He hurried on, aware now that the tide would soon be turning and the sea would come back in to fill the loch again. Once he slipped on a patch of seaweed and nearly fell. The urchin, shaken up, pushed out all his spikes again.

After that Hamish took off his big blue knitted tammy and, carefully lifting the sea urchin into it, carried him like that the rest of the way.

Down to the beach and the water's edge he walked, where the wind was lifting fresh, and the green sea waves tumbled in over each other, crisp and creamy white.

The tide had turned and was starting to come in again.

"Right, laddie," came a muffled voice from the blue tammy. "This'll do fine. Just leave me here, and off home with you afore the sea catches you. Quickly now!"

Hamish turned and looked back up the loch to where his wee farm cottage stood, a tiny white speck on the green hillside. Already the sea was washing in over the sand around him, trickling and gurgling round the rocks at his feet, filling up the pools and rippling over the sand. In no time at all he would be cut off.

"How do I get back?" he asked. "That tide is coming in fast."

"One good turn deserves another I suppose," said the sea urchin grudgingly. "Follow the sands. They'll take you home. Just listen to them – and follow your big feet!"

Hamish stood and listened. Above the sound of the sea and the gulls crying in the wind, he could hear another sound.

There was a soft, gentle singing that seemed to come from around his feet.

"It's the sands," said the sea urchin. "They're aye covered with the sea, but they belong to the land. They'll take you back to it. Goodbye now, and thank you. You're not a bad lad – in spite of your big boots."

Hamish watched as the wee waves lapped around and over the sea urchin, welcoming him home. Then he turned and walked back across the sand, following the sweet wild singing little tune. Sometimes it seemed to come from his right, sometimes it was to the left of him. But always it was ahead, leading him through the rocks and pools, back towards the white cottage on the hillside. And as he walked the sea rippled in behind him.

At last Hamish stepped from the sand to the seaweed and rocks of the beach beneath his own two green fields. He turned and watched as the water washed away his last steps from the place where no man had ever walked before.

And as he watched, the tumbling waves curled back leaving a beautiful seashell lying at his feet.

It was pink and white, rounded to the shape of Hamish's two big hands, with a smooth rippling pattern, like the waves on a summer sea.

Hamish shook out the water, held the shell to his ear, and listened. Far away, as if from a great blue distance, there came to him the sound of the singing sands, leading him home safely to Mirren.

6.
Mirren and the Fairy Blanket

Spring had come early to Camusbuie.

Hamish had dug over the warm brown earth, and he and Mirren spent long days working in the garden by the cottage planting cabbages, carrots, turnips and bright summer flowers.

There was only one task left now before summer came, and that was the shearing. Each year the heavy grey winter coats that had kept the sheep warm through the dark freezing months had to be cut short. This done, Hamish took the sheep back up the hill to the high summer pasture while Mirren prepared the fleeces and spun the wool that would make warm clothes for the next winter.

"This year," said Mirren as she washed the thick soft fleece, "I shall make us a fine new blanket that will hold us warm and snug through all the long cold nights."

"Grand idea," said Hamish. "And make it long enough so that my feet don't stick out at the bottom of the bed!"

On Monday morning, as soon as Hamish had left for the high pasture, Mirren set to work.

The fleeces were tangled and matted and she sat by the fireside with her two wooden carding bats, pulling the wool backwards and forwards through the spikes, teasing out the knots. Mirren brushed and pulled, brushed and rolled until at last she had baskets full of fine soft fluff, all ready for the spinning.

On Tuesday, Wednesday and Thursday Mirren sat at her spinning wheel, drawing the white fluff into a strong thread. She twisted and spun the thread onto wooden bobbins. And as each bobbin filled with the soft thick strands of wool, Mirren replaced it with an empty one. She sang as she spun:

"Hurrum, hurrum,
Turn, wheel, turn,
Spin a bonny bobbin,
Turn, wheel, turn."

Day after day the wheel turned, until at last all the bobbins were full.

Then Mirren lit a fire in the farmyard and set on it a huge iron cauldron full of water. She gathered together mosses and roots and as she stirred them in, the water turned a rich orange colour.

"We must dye the wool," said Mirren. She took the bobbins and with the help of Hamish's mother wound the yarn into loose hanks. When the pot was steaming and bubbling gently, Mirren stirred in the hanks and left them to soak in the orange coloured water.

When she judged that the first batch was ready, Mirren fished it out of the hot water with a stick and spread the hanks to dry on the spiky fingers of the gorse bushes on the hillside behind the house. And so she went on winding, dyeing and spreading the golden orange wool to dry in the sunlight.

It was while she was spreading out the third batch that Mirren noticed that some of the first hanks seemed to be missing.

"The wind must have taken them," she thought. But it was a still, warm, windless day.

"Perhaps Hamish's mother has them," thought Mirren. But the old lady shook her head. She had been dozing in the sunshine by the door.

Mirren counted the hanks of wool on the bushes again. There were fifteen.

"I will leave them tonight," she said. "And in the morning we shall see what we shall see."

In the morning there were only seven hanks on the gorse bushes where the fifteen had been – and there were some long pointed footprints by the bushes.

"So-ho," said Mirren. "Now who could this be, I wonder?"

She washed and dyed and spread out a few more hanks of wool, but then instead of going back to her work she hid behind the low stone wall of the garden, and watched and waited.

At first nothing happened. The morning wore on and the sun rose high in the sky. Then just as Mirren was beginning to wonder if it was not after all a great waste of time, a small figure sneaked down the hillside and crept over to the bushes.

She was twisted and bent with straggly hair that tumbled over her face. She wore shoes with long pointed toes and an old dirty green cloak.

She was quite unmistakeable.

"Grizelda Grimithistle!" whispered Mirren. The nasty little witch who had stolen their milk was now stealing Mirren's carefully spun wool.

Mirren watched as Grizelda lifted some of the hanks and tucked them under her cloak. Picking up her skirts she crept back into the thick bracken that covered the hillside above the cottage, and disappeared.

"Hmmm!" said Mirren. "We'll soon see

about this!" Pulling her shawl round her shoulders and lifting her petticoats, she followed Grizelda.

Over rocks and streams went the old witch, her long pointed feet squelching through the boggy places, with Mirren following, carefully behind. Grizelda stumped on, turning now and then to look back. Mirren, flitting from bush to bush, followed her to the top of the hill, then dropping down on her hands and knees she peered through the long grass.

Beneath her, in a cleft in the hillside, was a small dark cave. By the entrance, on a wooden stool, sat Grizelda. She was knitting with a huge pair of wooden pins and Mirren's orange wool. As she knitted she chanted to herself:

"Clicketty clack, clicketty clack,
It's a fine warm blanket that I'll make
And little does Mirren ken, the fool,
That it's me has stolen all her wool."

She rocked about on the stool, howling and cackling with laughter.

"Well!" said Mirren. She was just about to jump up and go storming down to the cave when suddenly she stopped… and thought.

Everyone knows that fairy knitting is the finest in this world or any other. There is a magic woven into the stitches, and secret patterns. A blanket knitted by the Wee Folk is a thing to hold and treasure indeed, and to pass on to your children and their great-grandchildren, for it will bring sweet sleep and good fortune to whoever owns it.

Mirren remembered all this and slipped off quietly back down the hill, leaving Grizelda to knit her blanket.

All next day Mirren sat carding more wool and trying to think of a way to trick Grizelda into giving her the finished blanket, and at last the answer came to her.

Before she spun the wool she went out to the farmyard and, putting on her fine white Sunday gloves, she picked a huge basket full of stinging nettles. As she spun the wool onto the bobbins Mirren bound in the green stinging leaves. Then she dyed the wool as before and left it to dry in the sun.

"Now, Mistress Grimithistle," said Mirren, "help yourself – please do."

Sure enough when she looked again next morning the wool had gone.

Two days later Mirren crawled through the long grass to peer down at Grizelda again. All the hanks of orange wool had been knitted up into a huge square blanket and the old witch was just finishing off the last corner. As she worked she chanted to herself:

"Clicketty clack, clicketty click,
I've stitched my blanket warm and thick.
With spells and magic woven right
To hap me through the winter's night."

Then pulling the wool through the last stitch Grizelda threw down the wooden pins and shook out the big orange square. As Mirren watched, the witch pulled off her dirty old green cloak and wrapped the blanket round her bent shoulders.

"Ooo-OUCH!"

howled Grizelda.

"Yeeee-eeech!"

squealed Grizelda, dancing about in pain. She threw the blanket on the ground and stamped on it angrily.

"That's gey rough wool," she snarled, poking at it with a long pointed toe. Then she lifted the blanket again, shook it hard and wrapped it round her shoulders again.

"Aaaa-oooo!"

yelled poor old Grizelda, as the nettles stung her back. Tearing the blanket off she hurled it away down the hillside.

"I don't know what kind of sheep they have," she snarled. "But I'll not trouble to steal their wool again!" She grabbed her cloak and stamped off into the cave.

Mirren tiptoed from her hiding place and, trying not to giggle too loudly, bundled up the blanket and hurried home.

Once again she put the big iron pot on the fire, filled it with water, and pushed in the blanket. Then she took a stout stick and sang as she stirred and pounded:

"Stir and row, stir and row,
That will make the nettles go.
Grizelda's knitting soon will be
Safe and warm for Hamish and me."

And sure enough the green stinging-nettle leaves floated to the surface of the water, leaving the wool soft and smooth. Then Mirren carried the blanket to the gorse bushes where she spread and stretched and smoothed out the tiny fairy stitches with the dream charms and sleep spells knitted through the wool.

In the evening, when the blanket was dry and warm, and perfumed by the wild flowers of the hillside, Mirren carried it carefully into the cottage and laid it on her bed.

When Hamish came home she told him

and his mother about the trick she had played on Grizelda Grimithistle.

"I would never have thought of that myself," said Hamish's mother smiling, and shaking her head. "My, Mirren, but I think you're the cleverest one of us all."

"Did I not tell you that?" laughed Hamish, hugging Mirren and dancing her round the kitchen.

And in the tiny white painted bedroom the fairy blanket glowed like the sunset of a perfect summer night, so that ever after Mirren and Hamish knew sweet sleep and enchanted dreams.

Hamish and
the Fairy Gifts

7.
Hamish and the Fairy Bairn

It all started one wild night in January. A storm had raged all week, howling round the top of the Ben, and tearing through the trees around the farmhouse, as if to rip them out of the ground. Rain and sleet filled the burn to overflowing, until the water crashed down off the mountainside, roaring like a savage beast.

On the wildest night of all Mirren's baby son was born, and the floodwater of the Balvie Burn washed away the little wooden bridge, leaving the farmhouse cut off from the village.

Neither Hamish nor Mirren cared. She lay

happy and cosy in the big bed, cuddling her new baby in his soft knitted shawl. Hamish sat by her side, stroking the baby's soft ginger curls.

"Do you think he'll want to be a farmer or a fisherman, Mirren? Should I make him a wee wheelbarrow or a fishing rod?"

Mirren laughed.

"Bring me his cradle first," she said. "I think Torquil will be needing that more than a barrow just now."

The baby was to be christened Torquil after Mirren's father, the Laird.

Hamish had spent the summer evenings making a sturdy little cradle of fresh sweet-smelling pine-wood. Mirren and the old lady had filled it with soft knitted blankets, and for weeks it had stood ready and waiting by the fireside in the kitchen. As Hamish bent to lift it he looked across at his mother who was staring gloomily into the flames.

"What's the matter?" he asked. "Are you not happy?"

"Och, I'm fair delighted for the pair of you," she sighed. "But it's just my wee grandson I'm not sure about. If you had only made that cradle out of rowan wood when I told you, then the Wee Folk..."

"That's just havers," Hamish laughed. "There's no Wee Folk coming into this house. I'll see to that."

She sighed, ignoring him. "And that bairn with the red hair. The King's colour. The very thing they prize the most. I tell you, Hamish, he will not be safe until he is christened in Camusbuie Kirk, and that will not happen as long as the bridge is down."

"I'll mend the bridge as soon as may be," said Hamish. "In the meantime wee Torquil will be quite safe with Mirren."

"Hamish! What ever are you thinking of, saying the bairn's name out loud like that.

And you standing by the fireplace." His mother was quite shocked. "Do you not realise *They* are up there, round the chimney stack, listening for that very thing so that they can call the wee one to them?"

Hamish just shook his head and laughed and took the cradle through to the bedroom.

Late that night Mirren woke up. Wee Torquil was crying for his feed so she stirred the fire in the kitchen to a warm glow and sat in the big chair singing softly to him. As she sang, the wind dropped to a soft moan, and through it came another sound, echoing down the chimney. A strange, sweet music:

"Torquil, Torquil, son of Hamish,
Come away, come away."

The baby turned towards the fireplace, holding out his tiny hands. Mirren leapt instantly to her feet, bundling him tight and safe in the shawl. The strange, sweet music was all around her, filling the room.

"Mother," she called. banging on the old lady's bedroom door. "Mother, come quick!"

The old lady padded through to the kitchen in her long white nightdress, pushing her spectacles up onto her nose. She stopped in the doorway suddenly, hearing the tiny voices, and seeing Torquil's bright little eyes turned towards the fire.

"I knew it," she said. "They're after the bairn. Havers indeed! You just wait till I have a word with our Hamish. If he had made that cradle out of rowan wood when I told him to, there would have been none of this."

"Mother, what can we do?" begged Mirren as Torquil began to howl loudly and to wriggle and kick in her arms.

"We'll just have to find a way to stop them coming down that chimney," said the old lady. She poked about in the basket of dry sticks by the hearth and at last pulled out a little sprig of fir tree, still with the green needles on it.

"A wee trick I learned a while back. This may hold them for a bit." She pushed the twig through the links of the heavy black iron chain that held the kettle over the flames. The moaning in the chimney changed to an angry howl, then died on the wind.

Over the next few days, the Wee Folk tried all the tricks they knew to sneak in and take away the baby. Hamish's mother went round and round the cottage searching for ways to stop them.

She unravelled a red ribbon from her best

petticoat and tied it around the cradle. Then she sent Hamish out into the storm to cut branches from the rowan tree to nail above the front and back doors of the cottage.

For three days and nights the wind raged and the voices moaned in the chimney. Each night Hamish, Mirren and the old lady took it in turns to sit by the cradle, keeping a wakeful and watchful eye on Torquil. Sometimes the baby would waken and, howling loudly, reach out a little hand towards the door.

"Aye, that bairn has his father's voice, right enough," said the old lady. "The noisiest child in Camusbuie, but we must be careful. They're still after him for all that."

On the fourth evening the wind died back, there was a glimmer of sunset out over the sea and the black clouds rolled away from the top of the Ben. The weather was lifting and with it the raging water of the burn settled to a thick brown hurlygush.

"I'll mend the bridge in the morning," yawned Hamish. "Then we can take wee Torquil down to Camusbuie Kirk for the christening."

"I'll not be happy until then," grumbled his mother. She shook her fist up the chimney. "Away you go, back to your own folk, you little devils!"

A tiny giggle floated down to them.

"Impertinent craturs!" she grumbled. "You be sure and lock up properly tonight, Hamish. I'm away to my bed."

But Hamish was tired and although he remembered to push the door shut, he forgot to slip the heavy iron bolt into the hasp.

Late that night, when everyone was asleep, the wind suddenly arose in a last furious gust. The door crashed open, sending sparks flying up the chimney. The cat flew, squalling, from the hearthrug, and the enamel milk jug toppled off the table and rolled with a clang across the floor. The old lady struggled out of bed. Hamish jumped up, with Mirren close behind him, and together they managed to slam shut the door against the storm. Only wee Torquil lay peacefully in his cradle by the fire as if nothing had happened.

"Fancy him just sleeping through all that!" said Mirren.

"Aye, just fancy," said the old lady doubtfully, peering into the cradle.

Everything seemed quite normal when Hamish set out early next morning to mend the bridge. But that evening when he returned he found Mirren still sitting by the cradle, looking worried.

"It's very odd," she whispered. "He hasn't cried all day."

"Thank goodness for that," said Hamish, flopping into a chair. "Maybe we'll all get some sleep tonight."

And indeed the baby slept right through until morning when Mirren went to lift him for his feed.

"It's really very odd," she said. "His eyes were blue, but they seem to be green now. They do say a baby's eyes change colour sometimes. Is that right, Mother?"

"Aye, it can be," said the old lady, warily.

During the next few days, while Hamish mended the bridge, his mother and Mirren watched the baby uneasily. He lay, still and silent, and the little bright eyes watched them in a knowing, clever way. At last the old lady, who had been sitting thinking, put down her knitting and studied him closely.

"I'm beginning to wonder if the Wee Folk are maybe away with our Torquil right enough," she said.

"Oh no, Mother, surely not, we were so careful." Mirren stared at the baby, with his little, bright, green, shining eyes, and grew suddenly uneasy.

"If they had taken him," she said in horror, "how could you tell?"

"Oh, that's not so difficult," said the old lady, nodding her head wisely.

She went to the cupboard and brought out a large jar of her homemade jelly, dipped in a little silver spoon and touched it to the baby's lips. He set up such a howling and screeching that the china dogs on the mantelpiece rattled and Hamish, hearing the row from down at the bridge, dropped his hammer and came running.

"I thought as much," nodded the old lady. The screaming baby sat up suddenly in the cradle, his tiny face quite purple with fury, and the ginger curls straight up in spikes all over his head. "That's no human child. They've taken our wee Torquil and left us a fairy bairn in his place."

"But how can you tell?" wailed Mirren above the din.

"Because a fairy cannot abide the rowan tree, and that was rowan jelly," said the old lady triumphantly. "Our wee Torquil loved it. I fed him the odd spoonful – just in case."

"Mither!" protested Hamish, but Mirren stopped him.

"It's just as well she did, Hamish, or we'd never have known. But how are we to get rid of this creature and get our own wee bairn back?"

"I'll soon see to that," said the old lady.

She quickly slipped another spoonful of

the jelly into the baby's mouth. He screeched even louder, shot out of the cradle, flew three times round the room in a furious bundle of blankets and out through the open door.

"Follow him, quickly," she bellowed. "See where he goes!"

The strange little creature tore up the hillside behind the cottage, leaving a trail of blankets and a path scorched through the heather. Hamish and Mirren raced after him, with the old lady puffing up behind them, still clutching the jar of jelly and grumbling to herself.

"If that daft beggar had just listened to me and made the bairn a cradle of rowan wood in the first place…"

Up the hillside they raced. Up through the trees, across the shoulder of the Ben, and down into the Fairy Glen where the heather grew thickest and even in the hardest winters the snow melted first. Hamish raced on, following the fairy bairn to a green, grassy mound at the head of the glen. The creature, skirling and shrieking, burrowed into the long grass, with Hamish all set to follow after him.

"*Stop there!*" yelled his mother. "Have you no sense at all? Listen!"

They stood, panting and breathless, and gradually, as their pounding hearts stilled, the sounds of the glen came to them. The birds were quiet, as if singing in a whisper. The wind through the bracken was soft and above it came another sound, far beneath their feet, deep in the earth. It was the sound of tiny voices arguing, and above them all, the howling, hungry cry of the noisiest baby in Camusbuie.

"It's Torquil," shouted Mirren gleefully.

"Aye," said the old lady. "And I think they've stolen more than they bargained for this time."

The hungry howls grew even louder, the argument more furious, as she marched boldly up to the grassy mound and tapped with her little silver spoon on a stone as if it had been a boiled egg. The voices stopped instantly.

"You thought to steal away my grandson, did you? I hope you're pleased with him," she shouted. The tiny voices wailed in misery above the baby's howling.

"Please! Please! Please take him away!" they moaned.

"Aye, well I might..." said the old lady. Hamish opened his mouth, but she held up her hand to silence him. "I might just take him away again. On one condition."

"Anything. Anything at all," the fairy voices wailed.

"I'll take him if you will promise my wee grandson the Fairy Hansel — the Wee Folks' gift to a new bairn. Grant him your help whenever he calls on you throughout his life – and we'll say no more about it."

Mirren gasped: "The Fairy Hansel! They only give that to the son or daughter of a king."

"And why shouldn't our Torquil have it? He's as fine as any king's bairn, I'm sure." The old lady raised her voice and shouted again. "Do you hear me? What do you say?"

Wee Torquil certainly heard her, and bawled louder than ever.

"Anything! Anything you wish. Only take him. Please take him, and with him the Fairy Hansel."

As the voices died away, the glen whirled around them, the air was filled with a strange whistling music, which faded as the baby's howls grew even louder.

"Torquil!" shouted Mirren, recovering first.

Lying at their feet, still wrapped in his

knitted shawl, with his little face quite scarlet beneath the ginger curls, lay Torquil. Hamish lifted him gently, and the old lady slipped a spoonful of rowan jelly into his yelling mouth.

"Well, look at that," said Mirren. "He's smiling at us."

"Aye, and no thanks to his stupid big father," sniffed the old lady, following them down the Glen, back to the farmhouse. "If you had just listened to me and made the bairn a cradle of rowan wood in the first place…"

But neither Hamish, Mirren nor wee Torquil, sound asleep in his mother's arms, were listening to her.

8.
Hamish and the Seal People

Hamish had taken a day away from the farm, and gone fishing. He pushed his wee boat down the rocky beach into the water. Then, rowing out to the mouth of the loch, where the brown hill water met the green sea, he cast his lines and waited. But never a fish did he catch.

Not one.

Through that long hot day the sun glittered on the sea, melting the wind-ripples into a sheet of glass. Hamish baited hook after hook, dropped them over the side and lay back in the sunshine to wait. At last, as the sun was sliding towards the headland in the west he sat up and yawned.

"Ach, it's no use, the fishes must have all gone on their holidays. Time I was away home for my tea." Slowly, he hauled up the line, hand over hand.

Suddenly there was a tug, and the boat rocked violently.

"Mercy on us, whatever have we got here? It must be a whale, I'm thinking."

He yanked the line hard. It tugged back, pulling him against the side of the boat. For five long minutes he rolled backward and forward, as the sea creature caught on his hook gradually became weaker and weaker.

Hamish gave one last mighty heave – and the line broke.

"Ouch!" He sat down hard in the bottom of the boat, then struggled to his knees in time to see a long, dark, gleaming shape turn and twist in the water. A trail of silver bubbles floated to the surface as it vanished.

"Well, I never," he gasped, picking himself up. "That was a real monster I've lost, and my hook as well. No fish for dinner tonight, I doubt." He settled himself in the boat, fitted the oars in the rowlocks and pulled for the head of the loch and home.

"Help! Help me, fisherman!"

Hamish turned at a shout from the beach. On the sand bar by the mouth of the loch, shadowy against the setting sun, stood a short square man. The golden light gleamed on his thick black hair and on the soft fur jerkin he wore. He was small, but powerful, and his face was brown from the sun. Hamish hesitated. But the man demanded help and, stranger or not, he must be given it.

"You must help me, fisherman," the man called again. His voice was soft, but strangely commanding.

Hamish found himself pulling the boat

towards the beach. Unable to resist, he climbed out and pulled it up on to the sand. The man's eyes, watching him, were dark and deep as the ocean.

"Fisherman," he said softly. "You have hurt my brother this day. He is mortally wounded, and you alone can help him."

"Your brother?" Hamish was astonished. "I would hurt nobody. I am a peaceful man."

"That is as may be. But nonetheless he is hurt, and by your hand."

"But I have been fishing," protested Hamish. "And saw no man all this long day."

"No man of your race, perhaps. But you cast your line into our kingdom, without thought or care, and now my brother is hurt sore. You must come to him."

The dark man took Hamish by the hand, and led him down the beach towards the edge of the sea. Unable to pull back from the cold strong grip, Hamish shook his head in horror as he found himself dragged into the water.

"No! No, I cannot go with you. I must not."

The man smiled, his grip stronger than ever.

"Keep by my side, fisherman, and you will come to no harm." Wading deeper and deeper towards the gold path of the sinking sun, he led Hamish on until the dark water closed over their heads. Only the otters playing on the wet sand saw their last footprints covered by the lapping waves. Only the herring gull, swooping high above, saw their hair, tawny as seaweed, vanish beneath the waves.

Hamish gasped, fighting for breath in the cold water, and then opened his eyes in astonishment. He had swum in the sea often enough before, but this was different. In the enchanted grasp of the Seal Man he felt himself floating, flying almost, in a cool green world where he could see and breathe. Deeper and deeper they twisted and turned. Hamish held tightly to the cold hand in his and allowed himself to be drawn towards the far-off glimmering green-silver of the sandy sea bed. Shoals of tiny fish drifted around them, like a shower of raindrops in sunlight. Instantly, as if to a silent command, they darted off, all turning together towards a mound of seaweed-covered rock far beneath.

Around the rock, waving fronds of weed reached out as if blown in a gentle breeze. The Seal Man parted them, uncovering the entrance to a dark cave, and drew Hamish in.

In the shifting, flickering light, they were surrounded by black shapes who came and went silently. Hamish turned back, to find that they followed close behind them, blocking the way out of the cave, and still the

Seal Man drew him on, gliding through the green water.

"You will come to no harm," he said. "So long as you are with me."

They swam through twisting passageways until Hamish had lost all sense of direction, and came at last to a small chamber, so round and perfect it seemed to have been cut from the rock. A weird shimmering light glowed from an open shell in which lay a pearl, the like of which Hamish had never seen before.

"Man," he gasped. "It's the size of a potato, yon thing!"

"Hush, fisherman," whispered the Seal Man. "We have come to my brother."

In the centre of the sandy floor of the cave stood a large flat stone. It was draped with a soft cloak, the edges of which waved in the gently shifting currents, like a living thing. On the cloak there lay a dark figure, as still as death.

"Our chieftain," said the man. "And my brother. Please, I beg you, help him."

Hamish crept closer. The man's thick dark hair floated around his face. On his right arm the shirt was torn, slashed and bloodstained where a fishing hook had been pulled deep into the flesh.

"It is your hook and it is iron," said the man by his side. "To us it means certain death and we may not touch it. Only a human may free him." He held out a small knife, the blade made of pink seashell.

Around them the dark shadowy figures came closer. As the Seal People gathered about the bed of their chieftain, Hamish could see that they were men and women, old and young, all with the glossy dark hair and eyes of the man by his side.

He knew their stories well enough. From childhood he had heard his mother tell them so often. Like the Wee Folk, they were of the old enchanted world before the Age of Iron, and that metal spelt death to their charmed lives.

"I see now how I have done your brother harm," he said, understanding at last.

Taking the shell knife, he slit the man's sleeve. Slowly and carefully, he cut the hook from the torn flesh, while the others watched. Then he took from his pocket a little pot of salve, which he always carried.

"This is prepared by my mother," he said. "And will cure most ills. It is made of seaweed from the shore and self-heal from the hillside." Gently he rubbed the salve into the wound, and bound it with a frond of the healing seaweed.

"I have done what I can," he said. "Now I must return home, for Mirren and my mother will surely be afraid for me, should they find my boat empty on the beach, and my little son will miss his father."

But the man who had brought him shook his head, for his brother lay unmoving, with his eyes closed.

"No, fisherman, you may not leave without my help and I must be sure that my brother is well. We must wait." He turned from Hamish and crouched by his brother's side.

Hamish sighed and joined him as the dark figures shifted closer.

Through long hours they waited and watched in the pale light. Around them the Seal People sang softly, a wordless song that rose and fell in his ears like the music of the sea, until, gradually, Hamish fell asleep.

He woke suddenly, at a cry from the man who had fetched him.

"He is awake! My brother is awake, fisherman."

Stumbling to his feet in a sleep daze, Hamish saw that the man on the rock lay with his eyes open, watching them.

"Fisherman," he whispered, "I have much to blame, but more to thank you for." Hamish, speechless, shook his head. The man smiled.

"I know of you, fisherman," he said. "We have watched you, my people and I. I know that you would hurt no creature willingly. Return now, with my brother, to your own people. But, beware, and heed my warning. Cast no more hooks of iron where my people swim and we may live together peaceably."

"You have my word and my hand on that," said Hamish. "From this time on I will take heed and watch out for you and your people."

As he reached out to grip the cold hand of the chieftain there came a rushing in his ears.

Tossed like a cork in a whirlpool, Hamish found himself struggling in the water, as if he had fallen from the boat. He kicked out and swam alone up towards the light.

As he waded from the sea, the sun still hung, a half-sunk ball of golden fire, spreading its path across the water towards him.

The tide still lapped around his footprints, vanishing into the water from the wet sand. Of the other man's footprints there was no sign.

His little boat lay drawn up on the beach, just as he had left it, and far up the loch, in the blue dusk, Mirren had placed a light in the window of the wee farmhouse.

Hamish blinked and shook his head, looking down at his clothes. They were dry as the dusty summer fields.

"I doubt but I must have been out in the sun too long and fallen asleep," he said, scratching his head. "A strange dream that was! Time I was home to Mirren right enough."

He turned then to push the boat back into the water and found that in his hand he still held the little shell knife of the Seal People, while at his feet lay three fine plump silver mackerel, a gift from the sea.

9.
Hamish and the Bogle

Everyone was talking down in Camusbuie. Heads nodded and tongues wagged – but always in whispers.

"Did you ever hear the like of it?" said Wee Maggie to the crowd in the village shop.

"Hear it? *Hear* it, did you say?" Andy the postman looked around the other customers who stood with their eyes goggling. "Did I not *see* it for myself?"

"Never!"

"Tell us aboot it."

"What was it like? Did it have huge flashing eyes like they say?"

"And a wail that turned your blood to ice?"

"Were you not – *terrrrified?*"

"W-e-e-e-e-ll," said Andy. "I didna' like it much. It takes a brave man to face a thing like yon. I'll tell you, this was the way of it…" They gathered round in fascinated horror as he lowered his voice.

"I was coming home late the other night, round the road by the shore – past the ruined cottage…"

Hamish, who had gone into Camusbuie to do some shopping for Mirren, stopped to listen with the others. It seemed that Andy had been walking home alone in the dark, when suddenly, passing the cottage, he heard a noise behind him:

HOOOOOO-HOOOOO!
HOOOOOO-EEEEEECH!
OOOOOH!

"It was bloodcurdling right enough," whispered Andy. "And when I looked round, there was the ghost – a great white bogle, wailing and moaning…"

"Aaaaaaah!" They were pop-eyed with excitement in the shop.

"…flitting in and out among the trees by the old ruined cottage. I stopped to get a better look at him and, guess what – he vanished clean through the wall."

"Mercy on us, Andy," gasped Wee Maggie behind the counter. "That's enough to give anyone the heebie-jeebies."

Andy was not the only person to have seen the bogle. There were others in the village who had seen it, and heard it, too. Indeed, it was getting so bad that nobody would go out after dark at all for fear of meeting the ghost.

That evening, Hamish told Mirren and his mother the story.

"Och, hoots and havers!" said his mother. "Ghosts and bogles indeed. There's some folk would be daft enough to believe anything."

"But I thought *you* believed in ghosts and Wee Folk," said Mirren.

"Wee Folk, yes. Anyone with half a brain kens aboot them. But bogles? I've never heard such clishmaclavers. They'll have forgotten about it in a week. You mark my words."

But the bogle was not forgotten about so easily. And the stories went on until at last Hamish felt he had to find out the truth for himself.

One night, after Mirren and his mother had gone to bed, and wee Torquil was sound asleep in his cradle, Hamish crept out of bed. He tiptoed out of the house in his socks and pulled the door shut behind him. Then he put his boots on and marched off down the road to the ruined cottage.

It was a still black night with not a breath of wind. The moon was a thin slice of silver, and even the stars seemed dull and misty. The only sounds were the soft pad-pad of Hamish's feet on the road and the swish of the grass as he passed.

He walked faster and faster. In the darkness the trees and bushes that he knew so well seemed to change shape and to move around him. Hamish was nervous and almost running as he came to the bend in the road that led towards the shore and the old, roofless, ruined cottage. Hunched and black, the empty chimney pointed like a finger to the clouds drifting across the moon.

He held his breath and listened to the silence. There was nothing.

Nothing but his own heart beating softly:

Putta-Putta-Putta.

Nothing.

Then suddenly from behind him there came a terrible noise:

HOOOOOO-HOOOOO! HOOOOOO-EEEEEECH! OOOOOH!

Hamish whirled round in time to see a huge white shape flitting through the trees by the cottage. He stepped back and swallowed hard. It was now or never.

"Aye," he said, lifting his cap. "It's a fine night for a walk."

"HOOOOOOOOO, EH?"

The white shape stopped whirling and flopped to a halt in front of him. Hamish stepped back and smiled bravely.

"I said it's a fine night for a walk. And get on, you daft big bogle. I'm no' feared for you."

The bogle suddenly shot straight backwards, clear through the wall of the cottage, and then trickled back again, like steam from a kettle spout.

"Here, that's a right clever trick," said Hamish. "You're no' such a daft big bogle after all. Go on. Let's see you do it again."

The bogle whirled back to the wall, gathering itself up into a ball of mist. But then instead of going through, it bounced off and fell – flump – like a large untidy bundle of washing, into a clump of nettles.

"HOOOOOO-ROOOOOO-EEEEEECH!"

wailed the bogle.

"Here, I hope you din't hurt yourself, your bogleship," said Hamish, most concerned.

"It's nae u-u-u-use!" wailed the bogle in a sad, hollow voice. "You're putting me off.

You're supposed to be terrified."

"Och, I'm sorry," laughed Hamish. He was beginning to enjoy himself. "Would it help if I pretended? Here, mind you don't tear your – em – thing." The bogle was struggling to untangle himself from a bramble bush he had fallen into.

"Ach, but you're no' really feared, are you?" sighed the bogle, with a sob in its voice.

"Well – to be honest, no," admitted Hamish. "The way they were talking down at Wee Maggie's I was expecting something really horrible – and you're not that bad."

"I'm no use at all," moaned the bogle. "N-o-o-o u-u-u-use." His voice was sad as the winter wind. "I'm just no good at this. I might as well give up and go home. But I haven't got a h-o-o-o-o-me." He rolled himself up into an untidy ball, groaning and moaning horribly.

"How's that then?" said Hamish. The bogle unwound and wisped himself up a tree.

"Well, it's like this," he wailed. "I used to be dead happy, hanging aboot in the old hoose up on the Ben there. I had a great time hurroooing and haunting for aboot three hundred years. But it was an old, old hoose and it just fell tae bits. Naebody would come up and mend it because it was haunted, you see. It got awful cold and windy up there for a poor old bogle…"

"So now you're looking for another wee cottage to haunt?"

"Right you are, pal," said the bogle. "I thought this would be just the ticket, but it's just as draughty. That wind's gey cauld some nights. It's no' good for my roo-oo-oo-matissum!" He stretched out and drifted around Hamish like a thin bank of wet fog.

"Right enough, I can see the problem," said Hamish as the bogle settled in a heap at his feet. "You have to find somewhere. Look, I tell you what. You just haunt about here for a wee while longer, and I'll see if I can fix you up with something better."

"Hooooooooo, yir a real pal!" wailed the bogle, vanishing altogether in his excitement.

"Don't mention it," said Hamish to the empty air. "I'll be seeing you – wherever you are."

Next morning, over breakfast, he told Mirren and his old mother the sad story of the bogle.

"He's not coming here," said his old mother firmly.

"But mother, I thought you didn't believe in bogles!" said Hamish.

"Neither I do. Stuff and rubbish. But he's still no' coming all the same." She sniffed and pulled her shawl tighter around her shoulders.

"Och, poor old soul," said Mirren, who was always kindhearted. "Maybe he could have a wee corner of the barn."

"He's no' coming here!" said the old lady, firmly. "Not even to the barn. The hens would never lay another egg with that thing dreeping in and out."

Hamish had to agree with her.

"Och, poor old bogle," said Mirren, spooning porridge into Torquil. "I suppose there's just nobody has any use for him at all... Here, just a minute though." She stopped and smiled. "I've had an idea."

The next day Mirren was up early and dressed in her good stout shoes and a warm skirt. She bundled Torquil up and hitched the wee pony to the cart.

"I'm away to see my faither for a day or so," she said. "You tell yon bogle no' tae worry. I'll be back soon."

"Flibbertigibbet!" grumbled the old lady,

who was left to wash up the breakfast dishes. But Mirren was away off up the high road to the castle before anyone could stop her.

Mirren's father, the Laird, was delighted to see his favourite daughter and even more delighted to see his wee grandson.

"And how are things these days, faither?" Mirren asked when they had settled down over a cup of tea.

"Och, not bad. Not bad. Awful quiet though, Mirren. We're not getting nearly as many tourists round the castle as we used to. Hardly sold a postcard all year. I'm going to have to do something about it, though goodness knows what. But never mind that, my dear, let's hear all your crack."

So Mirren told her father all the gossip about Hamish, Camusbuie, the farm – and the bogle.

"And I was just thinking, faither, you've some fine big empty rooms in the castle.

He could do a rare job haunting them for you."

"A bogle! In my castle!" The Laird was a wee bit taken aback. "I don't know about that, Mirren. It might put the cook off and, goodness knows, she's bad enough."

"Och, faither, he wouldn't need to haunt the kitchens. You could have him in the dungeons if you wanted."

"In the dungeons? Aye – well – maybe." The Laird stopped and thought about it. "Here, Mirren, you're brilliant. Maybe that's what the castle needs. A real bogle! My very own haunted dungeon. Noo, there's a thought…"

So it came about that the bogle was invited to move into the warm dry dungeon beneath the Laird's castle. The Laird got a grant from the Tourist Office to put up some new signs and very soon word spread. People came from far and wide to see the haunted dungeon for themselves. The Laird organised all-year-round Hallowe'en parties and the bogle had a rare time vanishing in and out through the walls, shaking chains and generally putting on such a show that everyone went home boasting about how terrified they had been.

Hamish's old mother was right too.

Within a week everyone had forgotten that the old cottage was ever haunted and, in no time at all, Camusbuie went back to being the quiet and peaceful wee village it had always been.

10.
Hamish and the Green Mist

It had been a long cold winter. The snow had lain thick on the tops of the hills around Camusbuie for weeks. The burn was a thin trickle of black water between hanging banks of ice, frozen into fantastic shapes. The fields were hard as stone and Hamish had to keep the cows in the byre and feed them on the hay stored through the long days of late summer. He came stamping in from the yard one morning, kicking the snow from his boots, his breath like a dragon's in the cold air.

"Spring's late this year," he gasped. "You'd

have thought the snow would have begun to melt by now."

"Aye," said his mother. "I don't remember when we had such a long winter." As if to agree with her, a bank of heavy black clouds rolled down from the top of the Ben. The hillside and trees above the farmhouse vanished in a swirling blizzard.

Week after week it went on. Everyone agreed they had never seen a winter like it. There was no sign of the ground thawing, no chance to plough or dig and plant the seeds for the summer. Down in Camusbuie they could talk of nothing else and, in the freezing air, there was no trace of the soft green mist of the first day of spring.

The old lady listened to Hamish

complaining over and over, until at last she had had enough.

"You can sit there and moan until you're blue in the face, Hamish, but I doubt if spring will return until you see to it yourself."

"See to it myself? What on earth do you mean, mither? You ken fine spring and winter, aye and summer too, come and go on their own."

"And there's whiles they need a wee bit help, Hamish. I mind fine one winter your father had to do that. He climbed the Ben and I saw neither hide nor hair of him for two days. But when he came back down, the Green Mist followed him and – oh my, but that was a bonny summer." She put down her knitting and smiled. "That was the year you were born."

But Hamish was not listening. He was pulling on his heavy leather jerkin, and climbing into his big boots.

"I'll be back as soon as I can," he shouted and trudged off, out into the cold.

It was hard work climbing the Ben. The snow had drifted deep and it was as if Hamish was a tiny creature, struggling to cross the soft quilt of a giant's bed. With every footstep, he sank up to the knees.

No longer able to see where he was or find the path, he climbed higher and higher through the thick blizzard. The driving snow lashed his face and there was a great roaring in the air ahead of him. Clinging on with his fingers, he crawled the last few yards to the mountain top and struggled slowly to his feet. The wind seized at him like a ferocious dog tearing at a bone. On the sheet of thick ice his boots were useless and he went flying, head over heels down the frozen slopes of the far side. Over and over he tumbled, round and round, down and down the mountainside, until at last he fell into a thick bank of snow.

The frozen crust crumbled beneath him and Hamish fell...

rumblede *thump!*

...into a white snow cave around the gnarled roots of an old tree. He rolled over and sat up, rubbing his elbow. High above him the wind raged across the hole through which he had fallen.

"You might have warned me you were coming," grumbled a crotchety voice behind him. Hamish spun round. Bright eyes glittered in the darkness beneath the tree roots. Was it a wolf? Or worse?

"I beg your pardon," he said. "I didn't exactly mean to drop in on you like that!"

"Stuff'n'puff!" snarled the crotchety voice again. "I expect They sent you to annoy me. They're always at it, the pair of them." A small man in a very scruffy green suit crawled from a tunnel in the snow and sat cross-legged, staring rudely at Hamish.

"Nobody sent me," said Hamish, brushing

himself down. "I came on my own. And who's 'They' anyway?"

The little man crossed his arms above his very round stomach, and sniffed rudely.

"Don't tell me you don't know!" he said. "Or maybe you hadn't noticed there's a war on again."

"I've no idea what you're talking about," said Hamish. "I came up here to try to do something about the winter and…"

"That's what I mean," the wee man squeaked in outrage. "They're at it again and they don't care who gets in the way. I should have been out of here and down the mountain weeks ago. But here we go again. His High and Mighty Maister of the Ice and the Great Laird of the Gales himself battering away as if nobody else mattered: 'I'm the greatest', 'No you're not!'"

The little man hopped around in a fury. "I'm telling you – whoever you are – their mother should have banged their heads together when they were just wee patches of bad weather!"

"I think I'm beginning to see," said Hamish. "It's all their fault. The winter going on like this."

"You're no' very bright, are you?" said the wee man rudely. "A right big tumshie. Of course it's all their fault!"

"I'll ignore that," said Hamish, trying hard to be dignified, "but how do you stop them fighting?"

"Make them think that somebody's won, I suppose," said the wee man. "Though goodness knows how."

"You mean, if the Master of the Ice thought the Laird of the Gales had won, he'd give up, and…"

"If the Laird thought the Master of the Ice had won, he'd take a tirl to himself and leave me in peace to get on with the spring weather."

"Well, there has to be a way," said Hamish. "Just let me think about it for a bit." He curled up in a corner of the snow hole and put his mind to the problem. It was not easy with the wee man sniffing and humphing and grumbling away to himself in the other corner, as he pulled together sticks and dry brushwood to build a fire. Hamish watched him crawl off into the snow tunnels around the tree roots and come back with more bundles of kindling.

"Here!" He grabbed the wee man excitedly by the sleeve. "I've got it. I've just had an idea."

"Mind, whit ye're at!" squawked the wee man. "That's an expensive jaicket. An' it's only four hundred year old…"

Hamish was hardly listening. He grabbed the bundle of wood and scrabbled around to gather up more.

"As much as you can get!" he shouted. "I need it all. And help me up out of this hole."

The wee man moaned and grumbled, but in the end he allowed Hamish to climb up onto his shoulders and passed out the brushwood.

"More! More!" shouted Hamish. "As much as you can get." He dragged the wood, slipping and slithering across the ice, staggering against the howling wind, and piled it on the top of the Ben.

Higher and higher the heap grew while the wee man tunnelled beneath the frozen snow hunting for more.

And still the gale howled around Hamish and the ice forming on his hair and eyebrows jingled like tiny bells whenever he shook his head.

At last, when the pile of firewood was the size of a small house, Hamish called to the wee man to stop. He crumpled some dry brown bracken leaves, then took out a box of matches. Shielding them from the gale, he set fire to the bracken and shoved it deep into the heart of the woodpile. The Great Gale, furious at not being able to blow Hamish over, raged around the mountain top. The tiny flames caught up by it leapt into life and snatched at the sticks, the sticks caught and in no time at all the woodpile was a huge roaring fire, melting the surrounding ice.

The Master of the Ice, feeling a break in his armour, came sweeping back from the north, his deadly breath freezing everything in its path. Far beneath he saw the wind whip the flames until they lit the whole sky and melted the ice cap on top of the Ben of Balvie.

"I have lost," he wailed. "I have lost to one greater than I." The hailstones that swirled around them turned to rain, pitting the melting snow.

Then Hamish turned back to the hole.

"Are you there, wee man? I need green branches, pine and fir. Quickly now. Quickly."

The wee man moaned and grumbled and

tunnelled like a whirlwind. Holes appeared in the snow around Hamish, and out shot great branches heavy with sweet-smelling evergreen needles. He seized them and stuck them upright in the soft snow around him.

"Help me, quickly," shouted Hamish, and the wee man raced around the mountainside sticking the branches in the snow until it seemed as if a tall forest grew there.

The Laird of the Gales, feeling his power broken by the branches, came storming down from the clouds to find a forest growing where none had been. Try though he might to rage and tear at the branches, Hamish and the wee man raced from one to the other, pushing them more and more firmly into the ground as it melted and softened in the heat of the fire. At last the Great Gale died to a whimper.

"I have lost," he moaned softly. "I have lost to one greater than I." The howling winds that raged around him died to a soft and gentle south wind.

As Hamish and the wee man stood and watched, the icicles around them began to drip, drip, drip. At first slowly, and then faster, joining the pools of water on the melting snow.

The clouds above them cleared and a Green Mist rose from the Fairy Glen and crept down the mountainside. Hamish turned to the wee man at his side, but he was no longer there. Rolled up in a green ball, he was trundling down the hillside. As he went, his voice drifted back up.

"Just as well I kent the right thing to do. Leave it to a big tumshie like yon and naething will ever get done!"

"Well, I like that!" gasped Hamish, then he laughed and looked around him.

Far, far below, a lazy thread of smoke curled up into the clear, blue, windless sky from the chimney of his wee farmhouse. He took a deep breath and sniffed the warmth of the first spring air. The white snow-covered fields would soon be ready for ploughing and planting, and the earliest snowdrops would be pushing through the black earth.

"Time for home," said Hamish. "There's work to be done." And, unfastening his heavy leather jacket, he marched off down the mountainside to the farm.

11.
Hamish
and the Birds

Tap, tap, tap. Tap, tap, tap went the noise at the window in the very early morning. It woke Hamish from a deep sleep. He stretched and opened one eye to peer out at the grey dawn.

"Too soon to get up," he said and yawned and snuggled down again.

Tap, tap, tap. Tap, tap, tap went the noise at the window.

"Hamish," muttered Mirren sleepily, "you'll have to trim the branches of that honeysuckle. I've been asking you to do it for weeks." She turned over and went back to sleep.

Tap, tap, tap. Tap, tap, tap the noise went

on. The more Hamish tried to ignore it, the louder it seemed to become. At last he sighed, climbed out of bed, and padded over to the window.

It was no honeysuckle bush tapping on the glass. It was a bird, the small round robin redbreast, who lived on the farm. For several winters Mirren had given him corn and scraps when she fed the hens, and in spring he had perched at the heel of Hamish's boot as he turned the earth, digging up fresh grubs and worms. The little robin was an old friend of the family.

"What's all the row about?" grumbled Hamish. "Away back to your nest, you daft wee chookie. There's people trying to sleep in here."

But the robin refused to be chased away. He bobbed up and down bossily on the windowsill, chirping loudly.

"Follow me, follow me."

"Away you go," said Hamish. "I've got more sense. I'm going back to bed. Shoo!" He shut the window firmly, and crawled under the quilt.

The little bird was not to be chased away so easily, he fluffed his feathers angrily and went on tapping on the window pane.

"Follow me, follow me," he called louder than ever.

"Och, see what he wants, Hamish," whispered Mirren sleepily.

"Aye – well," sighed Hamish. "I suppose there will be no peace in this house until I find out what it is."

He climbed out of bed, dressed, and went out to find the little bird perched on a coil of rope in the yard.

"Follow me, follow me," called the bird.

"I'm coming, I'm coming," grumbled Hamish, stuffing his shirt into his trousers and pushing his fingers through his untidy ginger hair. The robin fluttered uneasily around the coil of rope, sometimes settling on it, sometimes leaving it to fly around Hamish.

"You want me to bring it along?" he said, picking up the rope.

Scarcely waiting for him, the bird darted out of the garden, along the path between the fields and away from the farm. Hamish staggered behind, trying to loop the rope around his shoulder, tie his bootlaces and keep up at the same time. The robin bobbed from stone to stone on the dusty road. Every now and then he turned to look back and see that Hamish was following.

At the edge of the wood, the robin stopped and sat as if waiting.

"Well, then, what now?" said Hamish. He

looked around him. It was quiet and still in the grey early morning, a fine rain had begun to fall and the wind caught the high clouds, tossing them across the sky. He shivered, and scowled at the robin.

"I don't know what I'm doing here," he grumbled. "There had better be a good reason or it's no more crumbs for you this winter, I can tell you."

As they stood glaring at each other, another bird, a young chaffinch, appeared on a branch above their heads. The robin nodded briefly and bossily in his direction, stretched his wings, and flew off back down to the farm. The chaffinch waited to see that Hamish was watching and then, flipping from his branch, flew off into the forest.

Weet, weet,
Dreep, dreep.

His cheeky, chirpy voice echoed back through the trees.

"I can see it's weet for myself, thanks," muttered Hamish, pulling his jerkin tight around him. He struggled through the soaking undergrowth of the wet woods, following the bird's song.

Weet, weet,
Dreep, dreep.

Showers of raindrops fell from the leaves as the chaffinch fluttered through them, spraying Hamish, soaking his curly hair and running down the back of his collar.

"An' I'll thank you to stop dreeping on me too!" he shouted.

But the chaffinch bobbed on, leading the way.

"Wait for me, will you?" Hamish shouted, then lost his footing and slipped, slithered and tumbled down a muddy slope into a soft, squelching bog.

"Oh – no!" he gasped, hauling himself to his feet. His boots were firmly stuck in the sticky mud.

"I can't go on," he yelled. "And if I get out of here I'm going home again. You can sort out whatever it is yourself."

The chaffinch bobbed around his head, chirping loudly.

"I'm telling you, I can't move," snapped Hamish furiously. "I'm stuck in the mud! So it's no use you carrying on like that. You'll have to go back and get Mirren. She can pull me out with this rope."

And it was quite true, the harder he struggled, the deeper his boots sank in the mud.

"Help!" he shouted. "Help!" But there was no one in the wood to hear him. He pulled, and he heaved, and he shouted louder. And still no one heard him.

The chaffinch fluttered around in a panic and then, swooping off, vanished among the trees.

"Fushionless featherbrain!" shouted Hamish, hot and bothered and wrestling helplessly with the mud.

Lose two boots,

called a calm voice above his head.

Lose two boots.

He looked up as a large grey pigeon flapped noisily to a landing on an overhanging branch.

"What do you mean?" he demanded. The pigeon cooed softly:

Lose two boots,

Lose two boots.

Hamish looked down at his two big feet stuck in the mud.

"Och, I *see* what you mean," he said and, untying his shoelaces, he stepped out, leaving his boots firmly stuck in the mud. "All very fine, but here am I in my socks and what happens now?"

Soon, soon,

promised the pigeon flapping noisily around his head.

Soon, soon,

He headed off, up the slope.

"Aye – right," sighed Hamish. "I suppose I've come this far. I might as well carry on and see what's to do." He plodded on, feeling his way carefully over the uneven ground in his wet woolly socks, following the crooning pigeon.

"All very well for you, you can fly. My feet are frozen," he grumbled as he clambered up out of the thick wood, towards the high lonely pine trees.

On a branch above his head, the pigeon waited, watching nervously.

As soon as he saw Hamish leave the trees,

the bird spread his soft grey wings and, as if almost afraid to be out of the shelter of his own woods, vanished again among the green leaves.

Hamish stood, alone, at the foot of the rocky slope. Here and there on the way to the summit tall pine trees tossed their tops in the brisk spring wind.

An uncanny, eerie scream rang out, shattering the peace and echoing down the rocky glen. High above his head, gliding on the wind, hung a huge magnificent bird. It swooped down, blotting out the sun for a second, and then soared again, towards the pines. Its weird call rang out, sending other smaller birds hunting for shelter.

The great osprey called again and again and Hamish, hearing the fear in its voice, forgot his wet feet and climbed on, following the bird's vast shadow.

High on the mountainside stood a solitary pine, the tallest – and the last – of the old forest. Ancient as the hillside, it had been the osprey's home for many years. As a child, Hamish had watched, year after year, as the new chicks learned to fly. His father and grandfather before him had made the same climb, to watch the same nest, each summer.

"What ails you?" called Hamish, as the bird swooped and cried repeatedly. And then he heard the frightened voices of the chicks and saw that the old branch on which their nest was built had split in the winter gales and hung limply, swinging loose.

The little cradle of sticks rocked dangerously, like a lifeboat in a storm.

"Wait you now, I'll soon see what can be done," shouted Hamish. Looping the rope tighter around his shoulder, he wrestled his way up the tree, scraping his hands and face against the rough bark. As he climbed, he heard the tiny chicks

Weep, weep!

in alarm and their huge mother hovering above.

Hamish hauled himself up at last onto a high branch beside the nest, threw the rope across, catching the broken branch, and tied it tightly around the split wood.

"Hold fast," he shouted against the wind that whipped the treetops. "Hold fast and I will see what I can do."

He swung out, dangling dangerously above the drop and, pulling the rope tight, anchored it safely to the tree trunk. Again and again he looped it. At last, when it seemed to him that the nest was firmly wedged, he fastened the rope in three tight knots.

The terrified *weep, weep* of the chicks instantly became a hungry cry for food.

Tiny beaks opened wide as they forgot their fear. The mother bird, seeing Hamish climb back down the tree, settled in the nest to feed them.

Hamish stood beneath the pine tree, watching for a time to make sure that the nest was quite safe. Then, realising that he too was hungry and had missed his breakfast, he turned to leave.

"I'll bring wee Torquil up to see you next year," he shouted. "But I'm thinking by that time you'd do better to build a new nest in a safer place."

The great mother osprey spread the feather-fingers of her wing-tips wide and circled the sun above his head. Her high joyful whistle of thanks rang out down the glen.

12.
Hamish and the Fairy Gifts

With the spring came long soft days and milder evenings. Hamish and Mirren worked hard to dig and plant and sow the seeds that would give them food for themselves and their animals through the summer and the next long winter.

One evening, when the young grass was growing sweet and fresh and the garden around the farmhouse was glowing with daffodils, Hamish stopped to lean over a gate and look around him.

"Aye," said his old mother from the farmhouse door. "It's a fine sight. A real credit to you for all your hard work. I think it's time you had a break and we held a welcome party for wee Torquil."

Mirren thought it was a wonderful idea. She planned it over tea that night.

"We'll have everyone up from the village, and my father will come – and my sisters…"

"Do they have to?" groaned Hamish. Mirren's sisters argued all the time about how fine they were and who had the most money.

"Yes, of course we do!" said Mirren. "And then there's your cousins from over the Ben and everyone from the village. And what about you, Mother? Who would you like to ask?"

"Ah well," said the old lady. She had been waiting for just that moment. "That's what I was thinking. There's one or two that I think we really *ought* to invite." She nodded wisely, winked one eye and tapped the side of her nose. "You will know who I mean, Hamish."

"Och, Mither!" Hamish sighed, knowing just what she had in mind. "You can make all sorts of trouble inviting the Wee Folk in. Let's keep it for ourselves."

But his mother was having none of it.

"The Wee Folk were here before us and will still be here long after," said the old lady firmly. "Torquil must learn to live with them in peace and, besides, you will see the wonderful gifts they bring. I tell you, Hamish, they must be invited. You just leave it to me. There will be no trouble at all."

The day of the party grew nearer. The invitations were written and sent out to the family and the people in the village. The old lady went up the hill herself to see the Wee Folk.

Then for weeks on end she and Mirren

scrubbed and polished until the house glowed.

From early morning on the day of the party the kitchen was warm with the smell of fresh baking. Every cupboard and tabletop was piled high with scones, oatcakes and crisp buttery shortbread. Mirren set out cheeses, meat and thick slices of fruit cake. The big black kettle was filled and set to boil by the fireside, and they waited for the guests to arrive.

First to appear was a large farm cart with Mirren's father and her two sisters. Her father, the Laird, sat up at the front, chatting happily to everyone they passed. Her two sisters, in the back, could be heard arguing even before they crossed the bridge to the farmhouse.

"What do you mean, my dress looks cheap? I can tell you it cost a great deal more than that rag you're wearing."

"Oh! Is that so, well let me tell you, sister, dear..."

"A right pair of greetin teenies," grumbled the old lady.

Mirren shook her head, laughing, and went to admire the gifts they had brought for Torquil. Her father gave his grandson a beautiful silver cup. Her sisters had each brought a silver plate. They were furious.

"Why didn't you tell me that's what you were going to give the baby."

"Well, *you* might have let me know. Mine is finer, anyway. Much more expensive than yours."

"Oh no it's not!"

"Oh yes it is!"

"We'll ask Mirren which she prefers..."

Mirren was fortunately saved by the arrival of a crowd from the village, who came laughing and singing across the bridge to join the party.

Halfway through the afternoon, as she was passing cups of tea around the crowded kitchen, Mirren bumped into Hamish handing out platefuls of cake.

"It's grand, isn't it?" he said, smiling down at her rosy face.

"It is that, and have they not brought some lovely presents for our wee Torquil?"

The chest by the wall was piled high with soft woollen blankets and clothes for the baby.

"It's all gone very well – so far," said Hamish. "And there's no sign of…"

"Shhhhhh!" said Mirren. The happy chatter in the kitchen gradually died away and they all stood listening as the wind carried a little tune down the path from the Ben. Torquil, in his cradle, kicked his tiny feet and gurgled happily. The old lady leapt to her feet.

"I knew they would be here," she said

triumphantly, throwing the door open. She stepped out, followed by Hamish, Mirren and the others, to an amazing sight.

Down the path from the Ben came a strange procession. At the head, leading them all, marched a slim figure in a long green cloak and huge shadowy hat. He played on a little golden flute, and his thin fingers danced on the pipe in time to the haunting music. Behind him came a crowd of tiny figures, dressed in green. Some thin, some fat, some young, some old, the Wee Folk skipped, bounced, rolled or flew along the path to the farmhouse.

"Come away, come away," said the old lady. "And right glad we are to see you. Mirren, food for our guests, quickly now."

Mirren and Hamish fetched out platefuls of meat and cheese, cake and shortbread, and no sooner had they put them down than the Wee Folk, kicking and shoving, had cleared the food and were calling for more.

"Manners like pigs!" sniffed Mirren, but the old lady hushed her with a glance.

"Let them have what they will," she said. "And let them hear nothing against themselves. Fetch some more cake now."

So Mirren and Hamish went on carrying out platefuls of food and it did seem strange to Mirren that, however much she carried out, there always seemed to be plenty still in the kitchen. At last it seemed as if the Wee Folk had had enough. They lay around on the grass, laughing and joking, belching and burping rudely. The piper laughed and stepped up to the old lady.

"It is a fine feast you have given us this day," he said. "And in return we must honour our pledge of the Fairy Hansel. We would have you take this gift for the child."

He clapped his hands and two little fat figures came forward, trundling between them a large, empty, wooden flour barrel. They set it upright in front of the piper, placed the lid on the top and staggered off into the grass, laughing. Hamish and Mirren stared, a strange gift for a new baby, indeed. The man smiled, as if reading their thoughts.

"Strange indeed," he said. "But to your son we make the gift of a meal kist that will never be empty so long as he shall live."

Mirren lifted the lid to find that the barrel, which had been empty, was full to the top with fine white flour.

"Wonderful," she breathed. "Our thanks will always be to you and yours…"

As she said the words, the procession in front of her dissolved in the air, leaving only an echo of laughter floating on the wind and Mirren and the others gasping in astonishment.

A call from the shore brought them reeling to their senses. They turned to see a small group of figures, dressed in sleek dark clothes, standing on the shingle beach beneath the farmhouse. Their leader held up a hand in greeting.

"The Seal Folk!" said Hamish, recognising the man whom he had cured, and he stepped forward to welcome them. They were happy enough to see him again, but would not come up to his house. Indeed they would not leave the damp sand and stones of the beach between the tides, but they were happy enough to accept a little of the food and drink carried down to them. At last, when they had had enough, their leader held up his hand for silence.

"It is a fine feast you have given us this day," he said. "And in return we would have you take this gift for the child." He clapped his hands and two young men stepped forward, dragging from the water a silver fishing net, as fine as cobweb and sparkling like sunlight. Their leader smiled.

"To your son we make the gift of a fishing net that will never be empty, so long as he shall live."

Hamish bent to pick up the net, and suddenly found that it was filled with plump silver herring. He laughed and shook his head in amazement.

"How may we ever thank you?"

But the Seal People had already turned back to the sea, wading out and vanishing with hardly a ripple.

"What a wonderful day this is indeed for our Torquil," said Hamish, turning to his mother. "It seems that you were right."

As the old lady smiled and nodded, the air was suddenly shattered by a piercing shriek.

"I know that voice," Mirren wailed. "Grizelda Grimithistle!"

Down the road and into the farmyard whirled a green, evil-smelling cloud, which settled slowly to uncover a dirty little witch with spiky hair and a greenish face. It was indeed their old enemy, Grizelda Grimithistle.

"Thought you would invite the Wee Folk to a party and miss out Grizelda, did you?" she screeched. "We'll soon see about that."

"Mother!" Hamish was furious. "I thought you said it would be safe to invite them. You said there would be no trouble."

"Och, there *will* be no trouble. None at all," laughed Grizelda. "I've just come with a wee gift for the bairn. Let's have a look at him."

Before anyone could stop her she had pushed forward to the cradle.

"Ach, horrible!" she sneered, poking Torquil with a long dirty finger. "I hate small boys! But I've a present all the same." She reached down into the pocket of her dirty old coat, took out some green dust and sprinkled it on the baby.

"Here! Stop that!" shouted Mirren, shoving her aside. But it was too late. Grizelda took a deep breath, spread her dirty hands wide and shouted the magic spell:

"Eerie, feerie, tapsalteerie.
Cover his face with – measlie spots!"

"No!" Mirren's horrified shout rang out as Grizelda vanished, leaving only the foul smell behind her. In the cradle Torquil started to wail and rub at the itching red spots that appeared on his face.

"Whit'll we do?" wailed Hamish. "Mither, don't just stand there. You started this. Do something."

But for once the old lady was quite at a loss.

Nothing helped. Torquil cried louder and louder and his poor little face under the ginger curls was very soon covered in red measle spots.

Mirren picked him up and tried to comfort him. Everyone crowded round with a suggestion.

"Dab the spots with milk!"

"Rub them with butter!"

Suddenly, in the middle of all the fuss, the door swung open and there stood a small round figure.

"The old woman from the Ben of Balvie!" said Hamish, stepping forward to meet her.

The little woman was plump, with a rosy face and bright dark eyes. She too was one of the Wee Folk, and Hamish had met and helped her once a long time ago.

"Indeed," said the old woman. "I'm sorry to be late for your little party. But it's just as well I came, by the look of it." She lifted Torquil from Mirren's arms and looked at his scarlet puffy face.

"Poor wee bairn!" she said. "We'll have to do something about this." Without another word she turned and marched out of the house and up the path into the woods.

"Here! Come back with our bairn," shouted Mirren and, followed by the others, she ran after the woman. Up the path she led them, deep into the wood where the birds sang in the treetops and the flowers bloomed in the grass.

"Wait now, wait," shouted Hamish's mother, puffing to keep up. But on they went, deeper and deeper into the wood. Hamish caught Mirren's hand and pushed on. Leaving the others far behind, they followed the old woman until at last she came to a little clearing in the trees and turned to face them. At her feet was a small, perfectly round, dark pool, ringed with strange little yellow flowers, the like of which neither Hamish nor Mirren had ever seen before.

"Now we shall see what can be done for you," said the old woman and she stooped and brushed the baby's face with water from the pool. Then she picked a yellow flower and shook it gently. Torquil stopped crying as the golden pollen dust settled on his face. The old woman smiled and sang softly:

"Eerie, feerie, tapsalteerie.
Cover his face with – fairy kisses!"

A golden glow spread around them as she handed Torquil back into Mirren's arms.

"May your wee bairn always live surrounded by love," she whispered and kissed him gently.

When Hamish's mother and the other party guests finally managed to struggle through the wood to the clearing, they heard the sound of the baby's laughter and found Hamish and Mirren alone with him. Torquil was waving a plump little hand towards the trees. His little round beaming face was covered, not with spots, but with bright golden freckles.

"Well, fancy that!" said Hamish's old mother. "What was it she did then?"

But Mirren, turning to show her, found that both the pool and the little yellow flowers had vanished. In the quiet wood only the golden evening sunlight glowed on the grass.

Glossary

bairn: child

bawbee: old Scottish penny

ben: mountain peak

byre: cowshed

caterwauling: a loud screaming noise associated with cats

chookie: chick

cauld: cold

clishmaclavers: idle gossip

cratur: a foolish or ridiculous person or creature

dreeping: dripping or seeping

flibbertigibbet: an impish fiend

gey: very

gomeril: a foolish or stupid person

greetin: crying

hank: lock of material
hasp: the clasp of a door
jerkin: jacket
ken: know
kist: a chest or special box
loch: lake
mind: remember; know
mirk: dimness or dusk
mither: mother
nae: no
noo: now
skirling: a wailing sound associated with
    bagpipes
teenies: little ones
tumshie: an old word for 'turnip' and
    therefore an excellent insult
wag-at-the-wa clock: wall clock with a
    hanging pendulum
wee: small
yon: that, over there

About the Author

Moira Miller (1941–1990) was born in Clydebank near Glasgow and grew up in the seaside town of Ayr. Moving to Glasgow, an administrative job with the BBC led to her having short stories broadcast on radio, which she then expanded to create her first books. Over the next decade she had a successful publishing career while visiting schools and libraries throughout Scotland spreading her passion for reading and story telling to a new generation.

About the Illustrator

Mairi Hedderwick was born in Gourock, on the west coast of Scotland. She is best known for her delightful Katie Morag stories set on the Isle of Struay, a fictional counterpart to the real-life inner Hebridean island of Coll where she lived at various times for much of her life.

If you enjoyed
The Adventures of Hamish and Mirren
you might also like:

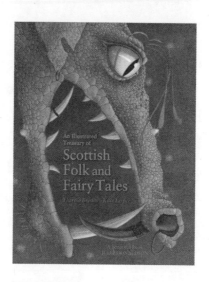

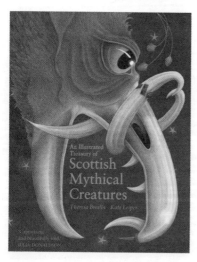

Praise for the
Illustrated Treasuries of Scotland:

'A lovely book with the most
beautiful illustrations.'
– ALEXANDER MCCALL SMITH

'A glorious collection of traditional stories.'
– VIVIAN FRENCH

'A harmonious braiding of pitch perfect
storytelling with illustrations of breathtaking
elegance and integrity.'
– DEBI GLIORI

'The illustrations are mesmerising.'
– CATHERINE RAYNER

'A beautiful book that will be treasured by
children in Scotland and far afield.'
– JULIA DONALDSON

Tales from Scotland's history

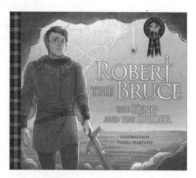
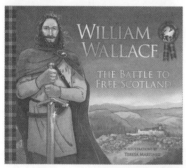
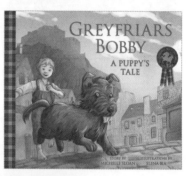
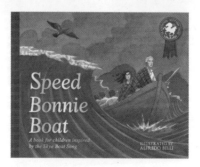

discoverkelpies.co.uk

Classic Scottish folk and fairy tales

discoverkelpies.co.uk

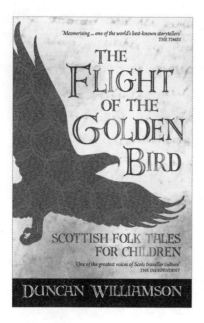

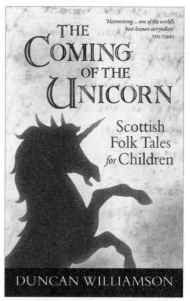

Two enchanting collections of traditional Scottish stories for children, full of animals and ogres, kings and princesses, broonies and fairies.

 Also available as eBooks

discoverkelpies.co.uk